The
Future
Was
Color

ALSO BY PATRICK NATHAN

Image Control
Some Hell

The
Future
Was
Color

A NOVEL

Patrick Nathan

COUNTERPOINT
CALIFORNIA

The Future Was Color

Copyright © 2024 by Patrick Nathan

First Counterpoint edition: 2024

Library of Congress Cataloging-in-Publication Data
Names: Nathan, Patrick, author.
Title: The future was color : a novel / Patrick Nathan.
Description: First Counterpoint edition. | San Francisco, California :
   Counterpoint, 2024.
Identifiers: LCCN 2023052623 | ISBN 9781640096240 (hardcover) | ISBN
   9781640096257 (e-book)
Subjects: LCSH: Screenwriters—Fiction. | Jews—United States—Fiction. |
   Hollywood (Los Angeles, Calif.)—Fiction. | LCGFT: Queer fiction. |
   Novels.
Classification: LCC PS3614.A863 F88 2024 | DDC 813/.6—dc23/eng/20231120
LC record available at https://lccn.loc.gov/2023052623

Jacket design by Farjana Yasmin
Jacket art © Jonathan Wateridge / Bridgeman Images
Book design by Laura Berry

COUNTERPOINT
Los Angeles and San Francisco, CA
www.counterpointpress.com

Printed in the United States of America

10 9 8 7 6 5 4 3 2 1

for Michael

My rose outside the kitchen window is flowering
for the first time. I wonder if it will see the
nuclear power station out.

—DEREK JARMAN

Paint, not line, is one of the clues.

—GRACE HARTIGAN

Los Angeles

WE WANT TO BURN, TO BE DISINTEGRATED, TO WATCH
our creations—the towers and bridges, the art, the machines, our
babies, our lovers, our dreams and bodies, thousands of years, our
ways, our poetry, whatever we want to outlive us—bludgeoned
and brained, thrown, crushed, but above all burned.

We meant everyone, George told me, whether they knew it
or not. This is what the movies were for. If you didn't just come
out and say it, the experience could be exalted—truly "out of this
world," as the posters so often threatened. You could know the
truth in your heart. But they always asked him for words—for people with names and pasts to run around and point at things or fall
in love. Every time, right as it was getting good, someone ruinously
handsome would step into the frame and recite a line George had
been paid to write—*The monster has doubled in size!* perhaps, or *We
only have five minutes to save the earth!*—and he was no longer in
that world, but thrown back into this one. Differently great and
terrible, as he described it. Differently burning.

He left. The film still rolling, no one on the sidewalk. The day's

heat had melted the sky into a syrup of an evening. In those days
there was a sameness to Los Angeles that nurtured rituals. The
palms swayed, the convertibles honked. The dusk bound the city
like gauze. He plucked a cigarette from the silver case. It was a good
movie—he had to give himself that. The hideous spiders, enormous from uranium, moved like they were alive, and the flames
that shot out of their eyes were believable. The burned bodies and
cratered cities would give people nightmares. Even the narrative
held together. But it wasn't quite *it*, not in the way he'd imagined.
They never were. *Death from Above!*: the poster was illustrated with
people in terror and in pain. It said, SCREENPLAY BY GEORGE
CURTIS. These films, Hollywood, America—none of it was anything to be proud of.

He wasn't alone. The boy or man in the ticket booth gestured
at the poster. "Wanna see it again, mister? I saw it this morning
and it worked me up so bad I don't think I'll sleep for a week."
There wasn't much of him—the kind of boy you could fold in half
and zip into a suitcase—but already George was transfixed. He
watched as he removed the stupid little hat they made him wear,
as he wiped the sweat from his forehead. A scar rose high over his
left eye like a second eyebrow. By now George knew he was staring,
and he felt arrestable, deportable. But you can't necessarily understand everyone with your eyes. The youngster pointed at George's
pocket. "Can you spare one of those?"

What smoking does is draw attention to the lips, the throat.
You can see how we are alive. In all the movies this was how the
stars entranced you. The boy thanked him—"It sure gets dull out
here by yourself, the flick still rolling and all"—and George smiled.
Some of us, maybe all of us in the beginning, think we're so subtle,
so secret. The film had another hour at least and the booth had

solid shutters to prevent burglaries, and everyone needs a break now and then. And the boy did have such lips. He did have, George discovered, such a throat.

═══

It was supposed to be 1956, supposedly autumn—even if California had nothing to do with such things. How else would it people itself? It even ensnared Americans, George noticed. And not just the Iowans and Kansans but so too the New Yorkers, the Bostonians, the Philadelphians. People had left real cities to come here, and not even to flee a war.

A few had done terrible things in what they called previous lives. Yet most of the Americans he met in L.A. seemed seduced. Even grown men—and not just *those* men—were as foolish and careless as the young, lied-to teenagers who ran away from home. It made their souls easy to steal and sell back to them, enlarged and enlivened. To trouble them. To borrow and make an alteration and return. And even George, after a drink on some rich actor's terrace, ashing into a pool among the thrashing, laughing, most beautiful bodies on earth—even he felt happily dead.

From the beginning, he tried not to know anyone. He failed. People liked him, and he, despite everything, liked people. Especially Americans. Perhaps because they seemed so much closer to dogs.

His favorite American was Jack Turner, one of two men with whom he shared an office at the studio. Because they worked together and lived only a mile apart, and because George did not drive, Jack pulled up in front of George's apartment every morning and honked. It was so wholesome. In return, George made coffee—stronger than you could get from any counter or café.

Every morning, George remembered, their lips sipped from the same thermos. Which wasn't anything Jack would notice; he wasn't the sort of man who'd care about lips. It wasn't incidental, however, that Jack was unmarried and childless and lived alone in a studio apartment on Hayworth, just before Sunset took its crooked turn. George had taken this into account immediately.

Yet there were years, he told me. Always years, like the sepia silt that gathered on silver and tarnished your reflection. But one day, some poor country's failed revolution polished time clean, and George saw, quite clearly, who his favorite American really was. Up until then, George said, it'd been so easy to believe he'd found a place to forget in—forever. But life, he said, is like that. It rolls along its boulevards and shuts its eyes to the glare of the sun, and then you're bleeding to death on some streetcorner where a road named after a flower meets another named after a crook.

It was Tuesday, October 23. All the history books would confirm it. A perfect day in California, but when wasn't it? "You'll need to call a car tonight, George," Jack was saying as the attendant waved them onto the lot. "They're breathing down my neck. If I don't finish tonight, you'll have to come see me at the soup kitchen. Or the morgue."

George searched for the right word. There was at least one of them for everything. "Coincidentally," was an incredible one, "I'll be staying late as well. A late-nighter for both of us." There'd been, of course, no such plan. A successful film meant the studio was already pressuring him for a sequel, but he hadn't made up his mind to take them seriously or not. *Death has come from above*, Edwards had barked at him, *so why not from below?* But there'd never been a good sequel in the history of anything, so George had turned instead to another script—something about an imposter. He wasn't

far along, and spending so much time with it at this early stage
would hurt rather than help it. Which didn't matter in the least.

"I think you mean an 'all-nighter,' but that's swell."

"Yes," George admitted. "We'll get some dinner, perhaps some
wine." The night was already getting carried away with itself, in
his head. "Or bourbon," he offered, "as all you Hollywood Jacks
seem to prefer."

"I like the way you think."

Jack knew nothing about the way George thought. At least, one
had to presume he didn't. Just as nothing had ever happened during
the day, with Ellman, their officemate, there at his typewriter, so
too would nothing happen in the evening. The two men—one
must never forget that he and Jack were two established adult men,
men with savings accounts and lawyers and references—would
chastely type, drink coffee and bourbon, smoke cigarettes, and
curse their failures of imagination, their shortcomings. Their mutual fear, George mused, of death. They would write the films they
were paid, modestly, to write.

Of course, with Ellman present there wasn't even the possibility of *something happening*, which is to say the possibility of fantasy.
Ellman was nearing fifty and wore bow ties. His wrists, richly ten-
doned and colorfully veined as they hovered over his Royal, were
like the dried little sheaves of sage spiritually enlightened actresses
threw into their fireplaces. He read Bertrand Russell on his lunch
break and maintained an angry, if sincere, correspondence with
the censors. It would be, George thought, like making love in front
of your accountant, if love was what you could tell yourself it was.
Even Ellman's movies were flops.

"Just once," he said when George and Jack walked in together,
"one might consider that there are others in this world—indeed,

in this very room—who enjoy drinking coffee in the morning." Everything he said, he never said it at you; he just unfurled it into the air like a flag and let it wave if it wanted, drape if it didn't.

"That looks like a half-full mug right on your desk," Jack said.

"Always the optimist."

"I will bring you a cup tomorrow," George said.

"One doesn't have to."

"This is true, yes. There's no compelling one, if that's what one means to say."

"No compelling one," Jack said, and turned to Ellman. "He got you all right."

They'd been together like this, the three of them, for two years. Occasionally the studio shuffled in a fourth writer, young men burdened with ideas who either quit or disappeared or got blacklisted. Men who thought they could mock McCarthy and get away with it. Men who doubted war. Men who said the word *union* and weren't even allowed to clean out their own desks; their possessions would be mailed, management said, after a careful inventory and examination. George had begun to suspect it was purposeful, these ambitious, feisty little failures flung at them as warnings. He was grateful; they helped deflect from his own oversights. Before the script that would become *Death from Above!* he'd proposed a film about an ancient monster deep beneath the Nevada desert, awakened by radiation. Why, they'd demanded, wasn't the monster hidden beneath *Siberia*? Why was it American radiation and not Russian that had endangered Las Vegas? He apologized. He was European, he protested. Sometimes he missed the subtleties of American politics. He congratulated them on catching his mistake, and appreciated their generosity in putting up with his foolishness. He was as dusty, he said, as an old library book.

"The word is *rusty*, goddamn it."

"Rusty as an old book?"

"Get out."

In his heart he kept a private script, never put to paper, where the monster was not only awakened by but fed upon American bombs, and by the time they finally listened to the scientist—a Hungarian, say—that the only way to kill the monster was to starve it forever through complete nuclear disarmament, they'd sacrificed half their own cities in attempts to destroy it. That, George told me, would have been a *film*.

Instead, this is what had happened to his life:

If he stepped out onto the balcony that overlooked the studio's backlot and connected all the writers' offices together, he could see a little suburban street somewhere in middle America, an Old West mining town, an outcrop of Mars or the moon (depending on the light bulbs), the imposing gates to an Arabian city. And beyond? Palms, donut shops, diners, and thousands of miles of dazzling cars laced together and draped over all of it like a gemstone shift. It was obscene. Sometimes, alone, he said, "I am in Los Angeles," just as he'd once said, in the same tone of disbelief, "I am in New York." It had become an existence. Even if survival's cost, it seemed, had ruined him in other ways.

Ellman had to leave, he announced, for a meeting. It was 4:40 in the afternoon. Jack waved without looking. George wished him a good evening. The studio had encouraged the writers, all of them, to keep notebooks in their shirt pockets, which were handy, management said, not only for ideas and addresses and phone numbers but for observing unusual behavior, should any, they said, exist. Each notebook had the studio logo and the official seal of the United States of America embossed on the leather cover.

The inside of George's notebook was blank. A moment like this, he knew, was what management meant by *behavior*: At 4:40 p.m., Tues, Oct 23, Francis J. Ellman left—no, *was seen leaving*—to attend a meeting. The word *meeting* would be, George imagined, in quotes, if not in actuality at least in spirit, and whoever read it would nod thoughtfully, knowingly. "Yes, a meeting." This said, no doubt, from behind a very large desk. "Thank you, Mr. Curtis, this is valuable information."

George removed the notebook from his shirt. He pressed it open, spine down, to the first page. He wrote, *Oct 1956: A woman falls in love with an all-American man. He is a robot with terrible intentions.* He pocketed the notebook. At five o'clock, he put on his hat, stepped out—he said—for some air, and retu rned with two sandwiches and a bottle of bourbon. "For later," he told Jack, and put on a fresh pot of coffee.

It was so shameful, all this over a man. It wasn't the first time he'd stayed late to keep Jack company while he sweated out the final pages of another war picture on deadline—something remarkably common in Jack's life. He knew, even before Jack did, at what time he would sigh and wipe his forehead and say, "I hope you don't mind, George," as he unbuttoned his shirt to the waist. And George knew how it would feel to look and not look. Jack, it should be remembered, was not young but he wasn't old, either—in fact George's age but better cared for, a machine kept oiled and tuned. Jack loved himself. Every few lines, he would give a sort of shrug or a roll of the shoulders, which only parted farther the curtains of his shirt. From thy clay, George thought, to mould me man. If you are like me, you are already imagining what George was imagining, and you already know why George waited, throughout their brief years of work together, for Jack to announce that it would be a late

night, and why such a stupid little phrase lit him up like a coal at
the heart of a fire given a slow, steady blow of life. And it is that
time now. Jack stretches his arms. He wipes his brow. He apolo-
gizes. He opens his shirt. Whatever George is typing, over at his
own desk, you can imagine it means nothing, perhaps even says
nothing. Lines of Novalis or Goethe hammered out from memory,
or Baudelaire, or Verlaine, or—God help him—Rimbaud.

"I know, I know," Jack said as he shrugged the shirt away altogether. Naked, for the first time, all the way to the waist. The
mass of his shoulders flicked and jumped as he typed, spasming
like a horse upset over a fly. He grinned. "Such a savage, right? I'm
afraid we can't all be as refined, my friend—as civilized—as you."
He curled a fresh page into the machine and popped the bottle
George had procured. "Pretty soon, old George," he said, and held
a glass in his direction, "the guys up in Mahogany Row will have
us all so overworked"—their fingers brushed as George took the
bourbon Jack had poured—"that we'll all be naked, roaming these
halls like dogs, grunting and sweating and typing up these stories,
no one to look at"—he winked—"but each other. Cheers." It was
after midnight and there were no other cars in the lot, no other
lights pouring out onto the balconies. Jack's feet were propped up
on his desk, his free hand resting gently in his lap, even if one finger waved, calmly, like something alive at the bottom of the sea, as
it brushed something sizably hidden. George did not move.

===

All of this was many years ago, and the expectations—if not the
sheer consciousness—of those living in America, or at least those
living whitely, had not yet matured or been yet maltreated into

being. It was before Norman Morrison set himself on fire beneath
the office window of the secretary of defense, and before American students were murdered, in Ohio, for protesting their nation's
bombardment of Cambodia. It was before the marches and beat-
ings of what would be called the Civil Rights era, and long before,
in the following century, millions filled the streets of American cities to protest its lingering apartheid. It was merely 1956. Only in
backward nations like Hungary could twenty thousand students
meet beneath a statue like József Bem's, in Budapest, and demand
the abdication of the People's Republic.

Within hours, the crowd had swelled tenfold. By nine thirty
that evening they had crossed the Danube, gathered outside
parliament, and toppled the thirty-foot bronze statue of Stalin.
They'd planted, George read, Hungarian colors in his boots. He
felt electrocuted as he held that morning's paper. Injected. Gassed.
He'd forgotten what it was to hope or believe, to imagine a future
beyond the pale headlights of one's aimless automobile. It took
everything to keep his voice flat as he offered the details to Jack,
whose own distance and malaise, wiped out after their long night
of work, was a relief. It was never wise, George told me—not in
those days—to let anyone know you wanted more than what you
had. As they departed their office and left the valley, the mountains were beginning to glow in the east. A new, terrible day. But
how, George thought, could you care about such trivialities?

"Three hours," Jack warned. He left him at the curb. Birds had
noticed the light. The most diligent gardeners had begun their
work. Tires were purring just around the corner, on the cool pavement of La Brea, and there was a wealth of crisp shade all around
him. Upstairs, things weren't so peaceful. The boy from the movie
theater, whose name, it turned out, was also Jack, but whom

George nicknamed Jacques, had taken to showing up at random if unholy hours of the night and demanding love or punishment. It was nothing they'd spoken about or agreed to—they never made plans—yet it had established itself through repetition, through patterns of sleep and tumescence. He even had a key, a copy he'd made without George's permission. They'd met outside the theater only two weeks ago.

Jacques was full of souls and they were all tormented. He cleaned the apartment for George and wore an apron when he tried to cook; he was nineteen and said terrible things like, "Come make love to your wife." To make love meant to torture. It wasn't enough until you'd bruised him. There were wounds up and down his arms, every stage from fresh to scar. He'd once shown George the pleasure, he called it, of extinguishing a cigarette on his thigh. "Never do that again," George warned.

That morning, he aped perfectly a wife's cinematic jealousy. He was furious that George had been out "all night," though who can know at what time Jacques had drifted into George's apartment to smell his clothes and suck up all his air. He was sobbing, smashing as many plates and photo frames as he could reach before George contained him. His accusations were tedious: "You don't love me, you're only using me, you don't appreciate me, you're breaking my heart."

It was ridiculous to speak of love here, George said. "What men do is not love. Don't be so perverse." By the time they'd performed their entire grotesque operetta with its betrayals and reconciliations and silences and lovemaking, George's three hours were up. As far as making money was concerned, it was now October 24. Jacques said, "I'm sorry for doubting you"; he said, "Fuck me"— words that always excited them both, no matter when or where, in their absolute filth. There would be no sleep. So George pushed Jacques's face into the sheets and went at him unrestrained, unshy about articulating his rage. Here, of all places, neither had to be on the lookout or remain half-dressed—only as quiet as they could stand. George beheld this landscape of bruises and burns and handprints and thought guiltily of empire. There was a place inside him, this boy, that shifted his voice an octave; you never knew which way it would go. Whenever George found it he pushed into it over and over and relished the sounds that came out of him, this boy who professed to belong to him, to be nothing, when in fact George knew there was an immense power here, a gravity he wouldn't be able to escape.

In the shower they soaped each other like real lovers. George was perhaps sleepy enough, exhausted enough, to hold him and to press his lips to his without lust. Under the running water a man could weep without shame. There was so much more to a life lived alongside another, even if it wasn't love. To place your skin in contact with another's, even if he was a man and the thrilling part, the meat of it, was over and done with—there had to be a way to endure it. And this boy, Jacques, he did have such skin.

Budapest in flames. New York crumbling into the sea. Los Angeles in ruins. The Soviets had rushed in with weapons but were not shooting. Nuclear war had come and gone. He was asleep and awake and dead but alive. Stalin had returned. Hitler had returned. Our planet was to collide with another. His parents had been abducted and lobotomized, surgically enslaved machines who wouldn't recognize him. The trains were running again—on tracks forged from bone and teeth and hair. The Martians would be merciless with our bodies, they would torture and vivisect and experiment. They would show us pieces of ourselves. Ancient beasts would slither out of the oceans and pull the entire city down into the abyss. The trains had never stopped.

It had been a deep sweat of days: newspapers, nightmares, drinks, double features, men. "You don't look well, George," Jack said. It was already Friday. At the studio George watched his type-writer as though it might write something by itself. How hard could it be? It didn't take much to pass as a script, not in this town. He continued to ignore the entreaties for a sequel and instead tried formu-lating a treatment for the robot picture, but he could only describe the robot's duplicitous all-American flesh in such detail that he had no choice but to take the pages home and burn them. "You should be celebrating," Jack went on. "At the beach last night, some boys were just *tormenting* this poor girl, telling her the sand was teeming with radioactive spiders. That pretty soon they'd take over the whole city. You've really done it, George. You opened the little door in their little heads and stepped right in." But what did movies matter in his life now? Who cared if one of his little fantasies—his bedtime stories, he said—got talked about or written up or even made money? He hadn't wanted to think about his home country in years, and now one of the world's great nations was out there being reborn.

"You always know just what to say, Jack."

On the balcony, he smoked and watched the production teams build and rearrange their flimsy worlds. Wispy ropes of clouds lassoed and whipped the sun westward. Whatever ends us, he thought, will come from the sky. California had meant itself to be the end, the paradise, the refuge. But it wasn't enough. It wouldn't be safe. We were a planet now, no way off or out.

What was happening in Budapest had destabilized him. Three days in, they were calling it a revolution. Stalin, despite George's nightmares, was still dead, but his haunted government had sent troops to protect the Hungarian People's Republic from the disgusted youth and their ideas. At first, the Americans were excited—a nation was turning its back on Russia—but when they learned that the young people and their intellectuals had given a list of demands, all of which would protect workers and provide medicine to all and offer educations to anyone who wanted one, that excitement turned into betrayal. These socialists, it was said, would get what was coming to them. The people had chosen their fate.

Even a happy dog, an idiot dog, has a nose like a hunter's hound. The Americans who peopled George's life asked him for his thoughts on this "revolution." He confessed he knew nothing, same as they—that is, only what he read in the papers. When they felt brazen enough to ask where he was from, he said as he'd always said—"Europe"—preferring its lack of commitment or association. It still worked, though he could see less of an understanding now, and in its place a flowering suspicion. *Good Europe or bad Europe?* He stopped reading in public places. He pretended, as Jack drove them to and from the studio, that he was too tired for the news. Which wasn't, he told me, a hard thing to pretend. He barely slept and felt feverish, damply paranoid from morning to night and night to morning. There would have to be somewhere for him to go, and soon. He hoped never to hear *communism* or *capitalism* ever again; he only wanted, once more, a home.

The nightly movies were supposed to annihilate his brain. He went to worship and to be destroyed but instead saw juxtapositions, and he analyzed them. Theaters south of Sunset offered additional distractions, but even the cocks he sucked in men's rooms couldn't obliterate him. He was thinking in sentences now. In structures. It was putting itself in front of him, a wintry tree flush with fat and lazy fowl free for the shooting. He wanted to write something *real*, something that would be part of a conversation. He broke an old rule and drank himself stupid. It was harder to guard a secret when you felt most like yourself, when you relaxed into yourself. You never knew what you'd say after a martini, and to whom, but it was worse, he told me, to be conscious, to be thinking and thinking of what would come next, of what kind of world, if he had a say in it, could be built. It wasn't, after all, like living in English; there were only so many people who spoke his real language and it was hard, in a moment like this, to keep yourself cut off from them, to withhold your imagination, even your wisdom, in a time of deep, dreamy need.

To paper over his long absences, he plied Jacques with gifts. He especially loved french fries, and if George showed up with a cone of them from the hamburger stand on Sycamore, even at ten o'clock at night, he could avoid an incident. It felt ridiculous and false. Whatever existed between them seemed measured in the calm between incidents; eventually, he'd have to get rid of him or leave him behind. It wasn't something either could sustain, even if Jacques was too young to know it. Being lonely was so terrible. Someone who smiled when you mispronounced a word, or who plucked an errant eyelash from your cheek—it would weaken anyone. You're just tired, George told himself. You can't think clearly. You've no faculty for judgment. In other dreams, different dreams, he and Jacques lived in Budapest and sipped coffee on balconies. They wore long coats and visited museums and lived, simultaneously, in the mountains above Los Angeles. They walked in the clouds and swam in the ripples of the sky. "You're burning," Jacques said as he shook him awake. Despite his youth, Jacques understood illness; it was clear that someone had nursed him, loved him, before they'd cast him out. "Poor Georgie," he whispered—only a pet name, but closer than anyone else in this city had come to George's foreign, forgotten syllables.

That Friday, he called Madeline. She would appreciate his pain, at least if he made it exciting, exotic. Jack had left early—he hadn't bothered to say why—and Ellman was little more than furniture. George let a little of himself out. "Let's say," he began, "that someone demanded you define love . . . ?"

"Christ, George," she said. "It's early."

"It's nearly five o'clock. Post meridian."

"Is that all?"

"No one ever thinks it's going to happen to him," he went on. In truth, George still didn't believe it *had* happened to him. He knew "love" here was fever and fervor, tangled in revolution—a young soul trapped in Hugo or Tolstoy, or some university youth with a tattered and cripplingly underlined Lukács. The politics of it, even the shape of it, had infected him with an adolescent's passion. He wanted to stand somewhere and make a speech people would remember. But Madeline yawned aggressively whenever anyone mentioned politics. Besides, it was never a good idea, anywhere, to be too terribly specific when phone lines were involved. So he blamed his heart. "I honestly don't know what to do with . . . her."

"Yes you do. I'm sending a car."

"Don't be ridic—"

"Call *her* and tell *her* to pack for a weekend. Swimsuit optional, as always. Drinks are at six thirty, dinner at seven thirty. I'll start getting ready now. Oh, George, this will be wonderful, thank you so much for suggesting it." She hung up.

George looked at the receiver as it mocked him with its drone. He set it down gently, a creature that might easily anger. Ellman had the faintest grin tugging at his cheek. "You have interesting friends," he said, then turned and winked. It was jarring, like noticing a statue or painting had moved overnight. He went on, still trying to make eye contact: "I have interesting friends, too, if you'd ever like to meet them."

George smiled. "I'm not sure anyone I know is as interesting as all that," he said, and excused himself and rinsed his face in the lavatory sink. Only an idiot would fall for such an obvious trap, he thought. But then what was he lately but an idiot? Strung out on nightmares and a bad chill?

Perhaps Madeline was right. Some sun, some sea. Vainly, he let his hand drape slowly down the contours of his face, the paunch under each eye that rarely, these days, went away, and the twin lines, like parting curtains, that swept away from his nose and out toward his jaw. As he'd watched Madeline do, in her vulnerable moments, he placed a finger at each of his temples and pulled up and back, only a little, and watched all those lines vanish at once. Then he let go, and frowned.

"It's so peaceful," Ellman said as George returned to his chair, "without that yahoo clomping about." If George's desk was east on their office compass, and Ellman's south, Jack was their North Star; no wonder, he mused, we are adrift. He ignored Ellman's signals, whatever they were, and pictured instead Jack's body, how the casual baring of it, the parading of it, stung like the opulence of the homes in Beverly Hills, or of citrus trees casting their fruit into the dirt. It *was* peaceful, George realized—like death or like growing horribly old. Jack was a movie; he made you want to feel erased.

Madeline Morrison cultivated mysteries. By her own admission, she collected people—those she determined were interesting. "You're so interesting," she'd accused George the first time they met. "We'll have dinner." It was at a release party for a flying saucer flick he'd written, and he'd scarcely said two things—neither addressed to her. She still, back then, had for George an angel's aura, someone who'd want nothing to do with his meager little world. By then, Madeline had aged out of the studio's preferred use for her, and most of her work came from long but sporadic stints on the stage in New York. No one, in other words, knew why she'd been there, celebrating a new mediocre film with the rest of them.

Later, George realized that her husband was, for his own reasons, inattentive to Madeline, and didn't mind her taking younger men as companions, particularly the sort of handsome, blank young men so often cast in the roles George wrote for them, and thus in attendance at these parties.

"You're sleeping with *him*?" he remembered whispering as they ate—or snacked, rather—on her terrace.

"Not anymore," she lamented. "He's with Walt now." Walter—the inattentive husband—had just stepped away to mix another drink.

They truly were, George had thought then, interesting people. He'd never felt so at ease, so unmotivated to lie.

Before Madeline, he'd never heard of Malibu—this strange shantytown of millionaires. Their house was a sprawling, Roman kind of thing meant to look ancient but was infested with appliances and electricity and carpet the color of cake frosting. Below the terrace and its heated pool, they had a quarter mile of private beach, and neither neighbor ever seemed to be home to spoil even that great distance. While George had never forgotten his commitments in life, it was the kind of home—if the word wasn't too obscene—that seduced even the most ethically resolute. "A person could be tortured here and enjoy it," he once told her, and she shivered with pleasure.

"So this is the one," Madeline said when George and Jacques arrived. Both were sullen. Jacques had thought George was telling him to pack his things because they were to never see each other again, and rather than express relief after George clarified the misunderstanding, his rage only deepened, and they spent their journey in silence. The burden of cheer was left to Madeline—which, of course, wasn't much of a challenge for her. "Your skin," she said as she took Jacques's hand and pulled him closer. "I've never seen anything quite like it."

"This is Jacques," George said.

"Jack," Jacques corrected. "He thinks the Frenchy name is funny."

Madeline smiled. "It's very funny, and so much more charming. In fact it's a gift. I do think you should keep it."

His hand still in hers, Jacques curled his fingers to escape, but George caught the little grin he tried to hide. "Thank you for having us," Jacques said—precisely, as though a child given strict instructions. He didn't recognize her, that much was clear.

The first martinis were ready and so were the next ones. Walt took pleasure in serving them himself, waiting until you took your first sip and nodding in approval before he moved on, a priest of gin. Unlike Madeline's, his career had not been forced into metamorphosis; Walt continued to appear in two to four films every year, most of them westerns and detective stories, and he carried

himself as though he never forgot it. Which meant he was someone you did recognize—someone Jacques recognized. Like a draft
of something illegally powerful, Walt left a person, an ordinary
person, not knowing how to behave or where to look.

"Yes, it's him," Madeline whispered in Jacques's ear, and pushed
him gently into her husband's realm. It wasn't until then that
George understood how it was that Madeline intended to help.

—

By necessity, George had a secret life. But he was also restlessly intelligent, and had, by choice, another. Only Madeline, and perhaps
the bookshelves and windowsills of his apartment, knew about the
second—something he'd confided when he still craved her esteem,
when he tried to seem as interesting as she wanted to believe he
was. These deeply unserious films—he was so much more than
that, he'd wanted her to know. But like all confidences, it turned
into a vulnerability; it made him afraid of Madeline, her fickleness.
George felt he had no choice but to tell her everything she asked.

"So what is it you're *really* working on?" she wanted to know,
once Walt and Jacques were deep in a conversation of their own.

George hid behind a sip of his drink. "I'm sure you've heard,"
he lied, "of what's happening in Hungary—the students' revolt,
the attempt at suppression, their demands and so on."

"Yes," she imagined. "It's all just so shocking."

"I'm putting together some thoughts, that's all."

"Some thoughts?"

"I don't precisely know what they are, just yet. I haven't felt like
I've had much time to think, to organize." In truth George hadn't
put a single word to paper—not on the machine and not in his

notebooks. He'd been trying to resist. To react, in words, to what was happening in Budapest would be to harbor hope for a country he left long ago. He didn't come here to hope.

He'd been struck like this—or called, if he was feeling especially exalted—many times over the last several years, if to a lesser degree and intensity. In New York, he'd written essays and criticism more regularly, more seriously, and had even tried to publish under the obscure, vaguely European *G. W. Kurtz*, whose byline never went beyond "Mr. Kurtz is a writer living in New York." Even in the rare essay George mailed from Los Angeles, Mr. Kurtz continued to live in New York—his correspondence managed from the address of a painter he trusted, and whose oily fingerprints on the rejection slips she forwarded conjured a grief it was difficult not to indulge. He could see what he'd lost. Honest, dirty sunlight in a long, cold room, where the water pipes and the air ducts, and even the sofas dragged up from the streets, all groaned at your presence, and where people talked, really talked, until four or five in the morning, and then talked some more over coffee, and meant what they said. The hot steam of the cafeterias, how you couldn't see anything but shapes out their windows, blues and patterned greys and strips of fluttering beige, and drips, and streaks, an entire wall of painted light. Was it any wonder, he thought, that so many of them had come to prefer color for color's sake?

"What you need," Madeline said, "is solitude. Some time away." A window slammed so suddenly in George's mind that he winced at its anger, its pain. She was smiling at him, petting the rim of her glass like a piece of jewelry. "You know we have the room, my darling."

"And you know I couldn't take it."

"Don't be ridiculous, George. You're really onto something, I'm sure of it. The world needs you, and it needs you *here*, not scratching out summer trash and fooling around with some . . . some . . ." She couldn't find the word as she glanced over at Jacques, or at least its less offensive synonym. "You know what I mean. You deserve so much more than what you have, and it's the least I can do, to give you some space to think and to write. Besides, imagine what you'd do for me—a real writer, creating something from nothing, all in my little house here on the beach. Just having you here, knowing what you're up to—it would be so interesting."

George finished his drink and made for a cigarette. She cut him off with one of her own and reached for the large crystal lighter she kept in a tray on the ottoman. Across the flame, her eyes glowed a satanic green. He knew this was how she seduced people. In another time they'd have burned her as a witch. But they'd have burned George, too, little bundle of sticks, so to speak, that he was. And a Jew. "What about Jacques?" he said, but he already knew.

"Yes, Jacques." She laughed and gathered her dress into her arms, unsinking herself from the deep corner of the sofa. "Walt," she called, and he snapped to her attention. She pointed at the bar and made a small gesture with her thumb, and Walt did as she bade. With George and Jacques, she was less mysterious: "Let's see how the terrace is doing, shall we?" she said, and guided them both through the large sliding doors of the salon and out into the night. Even the stars here were pink, as though she'd dyed them herself. And the moonlight on the water. And the jazz on the radio. An unmistakable pop came from the living room and Walt reappeared, absolutely naked, with a bottle and four glasses. Jacques turned a shade of red George knew well, but he didn't need much encouragement. He stripped and dove into the pool while Walt carefully followed. George and Madeline reclined on the loungers and watched them swim, and tease, and kiss, and moan, and meanwhile told each other their secrets, their gossip, their theories, their favorite texture of cake, where to buy croissants in New York, the things poets died for, and how he never in his life, George, expected to be here, doing this, seeing this, while the boy who'd called himself his wife, who'd professed, like an actor giving a monologue, what George would always mean to him, looked him right in the eye as this famous leading man spread out a towel, gave himself a generous coating of spit, and slipped into him from behind. Madeline had always understood what people wanted. She did have, you must admit, a talent.

THE RESIDENCY

He woke early the next morning. Jacques had slept in Walt's bed, and despite the gin and champagne and cigarettes, George felt wholly himself. He searched for a dressing gown, embarrassed by yesterday's wrinkled clothes tossed over the back of a chair. Instead, in the wardrobe, he found clothes of his own, including the robe he liked to wear in the mornings. Along another wall, he noticed a small stack of boxes—books, news clippings, journals, magazines. *His* books and clippings, his magazines. So too his typewriter, his notepads and pens. In his head, he practiced a speech: how he would, over breakfast, turn down Madeline's offer and return home, even if it meant hiring a cab. With all his things here and half unpacked, he wanted to be angry—Joe, as it were, to her Norma. But it was, he told me, such a beautiful, quiet room on such a beautiful, quiet beach, and despite the violation he felt cared for. Even protected.

Outside his room, there was no trace of their debauchery. No glasses on the terrace or in the salon, no bottles, no discarded underwear, no bundled-up towels or stains. There were fresh roses on the piano and a spread of fruit and pastries on the table outside. Now that he'd been spotted, a carafe of coffee was on its way. The ocean lay curled up and purring at their feet.

Much to his shock, he told me, he worked. It was providential he'd woken up early; by the time he'd had his coffee and his bread and jam and gone back to his room, no one except the servants—who despite his efforts didn't say much beyond *yes* or *no* or *of course, sir*—was awake. In his room, a desk had been set up for him, probably while he'd sipped his coffee and surveyed the beach, the mountains, everything in its morning tinge of blue—the only time L.A. was ever blue. Here, his typewriter faced a great wall of windows. It was like a postcard or a magazine, something trying to sell him cigarettes or furniture or a tour around the world. Madeline was silly, he decided. Her ideas about people were childish, dehumanizing. He thumbed through his papers, stacked neatly beside the Olivetti. *Ideally, we would not be human at all*, he thought, *but here we are*. Out of curiosity he typed it, to see how it would look.

All day, no one bothered him. At noon, a young woman brought him a sandwich and a salad and a chilled glass of chardonnay, and, when he'd finished with that, a fresh cup of coffee. The problem was violence—and who had the privilege of defining it. Which meant there were certain societal or cultural obligations to consider the experience of violence, the simulation of violence. Even, he thought, the *testament* of violence. As he knew, it had its own spirituality—which you could never neglect or overlook.

In between paragraphs, George thumbed through one book, then another. Each note in each margin suggested that he linger on that page, if only to remember what, originally, had caught his attention. Despair was aristocratic—its temptation to announce that man was ruined. What meaning was there in declaring, from one's castle, that life was terrible—that man had no future? It was a unique narcissism to say that life could not or should not go on after one's own life drew to a comfortable close.

That is to say, *as narcissism* it was unique.

The golden hours: some things earned their names. The Olivetti's shell had deepened and warmed, as though he could reach his hand into its black pool of metal and pull out a stone or smoothened pebble, or a little inky conch. Fans of oily light on the windowglass, his cigarette's curls like a cold rope of honey spooned into water. The day's—every day's—spilled cup of tea. George had been alone for eight hours. He'd read no news, heard no voices. He walked over to the window and put his hand on the glass. There was the beach and there was the surf and there, if you let the part of you that knew better go quiet, was endlessness. It wouldn't be so hard to believe. You could be old or sick and waiting here, at one of the world's last places, farthest places, tasting the breeze you knew or thought you knew would carry your breath once it finally let go of your body, and sail where only breath sails. He closed his eyes and pulled in a deep breath and imagined it, yet something seized in his muscles and he couldn't hang on—his laughter pulled out of him as if it weren't his at all.

George was happy.

It wasn't a bad way to end a day, and he left his room as it was. They were all on the terrace—these two movie stars and their na-ked adoptee, guilty and happy as he was. Madeline offered him a drink. "Have you had one before?" she asked, placing him in the difficult, if inevitable, position of having to inquire:

"One?"

"Oh, George," she laughed. She gestured at its seafoam opalescence, trembling in the martini glass like a little brackish harbor somewhere hot and milkily forgotten. "Hemingway calls it 'Death in the Afternoon.' You're supposed to drink three to five of them, he stipulates—slowly." In one gulp she knocked back what remained and laughed. "But what does he know?"

When he got a moment and the absinthe had loosened him, George sat quietly with Jacques while Madeline lectured her husband on the importance of offering, with dinner, a variety of cheeses. "You think I'm angry," he said. Jacques kept his eyes lowered. There were handprints on his throat and a deep, purple bite on his shoulder. Even now, George was captivated—and thankful that his arousal was hidden beneath his clothes. "I think it's beautiful," he went on, "to see you enjoy life, and enjoy it so . . . what is the right word? So radically. Is it too much to say I'm proud of you, my little Jacques?"

The boy began to cry. As if on instinct he slid over onto George's lounger and curled up into him, his head on his chest. "I just never thought people could live like this."

George laughed and took another sip. "With money, you can live however you want. It makes nothing matter."

"I want to have money."

"Yes. Even the rich want money. Perhaps nobody more than they." He looked at Madeline, at Walt. It wasn't the first time he'd imagined them ruined, even destitute. Their alcoholism and loneliness reduced to swill, to terrible skin and diseases you could smell rotting from within. To see them bent and broken, old before their time as all the world's poor are. Even if it were impossible, it was something George had conjured as an experiment, as a tiny, inner revenge. Was he cruel for it?

Did it matter?

Jacques would never be rich, of course. Nor George. They weren't made of it. He wanted to tell him not to worry about it, never to worry because it wouldn't matter, it would all be for nothing, and Jacques was good just the way he was. But no one ever believed this particular species of truth. He kissed his forehead, its sweet tang of bleach. "You are kind," he said. "That is the most important."

After another drink, Madeline announced—her own word—a *digression*. "What I mean is that I'd like to talk about something else," she explained. She hadn't been talking about anything.

Walt, sunk deep in his chair, gazed into the abyss. "What the hell is there to talk about."

She plucked her husband's lighter from the glass table and twirled it in her fingers, sometimes lit, sometimes not. Its little metal clink each time it snapped closed made George itch for a cigarette. Then she sighed. "Let's talk about . . . about dreams. No." She sat up and tossed the lighter on the table. "I nearly forgot—I want to talk about cheese. In fact I'd like to go shopping. George"— she pointed—"let's get dressed."

=====

Madeline apologized, once she got something into her head it was like a cancer, she had to operate, George would understand, and wasn't it, besides, a lovely evening for a drive? They sat side by side and she caressed his hand in hers. Yucca leaves, bony mesquite, stones in the washes like palmfuls of pearls held out to the sea. They weren't going far. George couldn't see the driver and felt ashamed; it was indecent not to know who carried your life in his hands. The *fromagerie*, as Madeline loudly called it, was just "in town" on a little street of shops—a gas station, two restaurants, a lineup of wooden shacks, all facing the water. If George understood her correctly, young men blew in from time to time like pods of jellyfish to ride the waves, shake the sea out of their locks, and start fires on the beach. "It's like something out of an old legend," she said. Her breath was astringent and George wondered over his own, too self-conscious to test it behind his hand. "You would appreciate it."

The cheese shop was more of a deli, though decidedly un-Jewish. There were salamis and hams hung from the ceiling, jars of olives and jams on the shelves, baskets of bread, and bins of shelled and unshelled nuts. But Madeline wasn't wrong—there were more varieties of cheese here than in any of the American stores George had ever seen. More even than in Budapest, though that was perhaps not the fairest comparison. The owner, she explained, was Peter Houghton, the actor. (Madeline always used the definitive article.) He'd fallen in love, she explained, with France, but then fell in love with California. And never cared much for his own England. But who would, after such places?

George recognized instantly what he and Houghton had in common. For a moment, he feared this was what Madeline had devised—first, lure him out to this middle of nowhere on the ocean, then pair him up with someone local. But it was only a coincidence. Or, more appropriately, an inevitability: Madeline liked a certain kind of friend and lacked imagination or interest in gathering others. Cultured men, as it were, men with manners, men of refinement. Safe men.

"George was just telling me how much he missed the food in Europe," Madeline said. "And I thought, I know the *perfect* place."

George smiled, and feigned a cough into his hand as Houghton asked the question he knew was coming—"Where in Europe?"— to make it easier to pretend he hadn't heard. A Brit would never, George knew, risk the humiliation of asking twice.

Madeline clutched his arm and nodded toward the cabinet. "Isn't it just like in Paris?"

Paris. What a myth. He wasn't sure how often Madeline visited, or what she did there, aside from eat and drink and buy new clothes. Nor was he sure, outside of the occasional photograph or film, what it looked like. In fact it was in films that he imagined her, as she went from bistro to bistro or café to café, as she walked along the Seine. The camera would follow her, trembling slightly with the cinematographer's flaws, as in so many of the new films. It was like her, of course, to have never asked—to have just assumed that Paris was part of everyone's life, or at least everyone she had in hers. Paris was just another thing to collect for people like Madeline—that is, for people who couldn't appreciate it. George smiled. "I've never been, I'm afraid."

He'd known, of course, how she would react, and there were a dozen other things he could have said to avoid piercing her mood. *That's what they say*, perhaps, or *That's how I always picture it.* But sometimes Madeline brought out what was most cruel in George. There was even a delight in it, to bring others low, to exert such power. She smiled at him and took a half step away from the counter, away from Houghton, as if she'd been caught associating with the wrong crowd. Then she laughed. "Perhaps I exaggerate somewhat. Maybe it isn't like Paris, or anywhere I've been. Maybe it's just like Malibu, or California, I don't really know. I never really know, do I, what I'm talking about."

They selected, on Houghton's chilly advice, two soft cheeses, one firm, a baguette, quince preserves, and a little jar of rabbit rillettes. "Made here in the shop, you know," he said. He had learned the recipe, he began, but George didn't follow the rest. It was a mistake to have let Madeline abduct him, to carry him around like a handbag, wear him like a scarf. Right when he felt called, when there was at last something to be serious about. He was shocked at his sudden rage. It dammed up his veins and hardened the flesh in his arms. He wouldn't be anyone's object, any spoiled woman's rotten little dog.

"If you'll excuse me," he said while Madeline paid. He flashed her his smile and stepped out onto the sidewalk, where he nearly bumped into Jack Turner.

"George!" It was the most wonderful thing he'd heard in days.

Their stories went like this:

Jack was in Malibu to check in on his aunt, who'd just had an operation—the ambiguity of which, George noticed, gave an authority you barely wanted to question. Doreen had a garden, Jack said, and it would break her heart to see it fallow. She had a monstera her mother had given as a wedding present and her mother was dead. It wasn't too bad of a drive, and he'd always meant to spend more time with poor Doreen, now that she was so alone; he only wished it were under different circumstances, that he hadn't waited until she'd rendered herself an invalid. "I'm sure you have family, George, so you understand."

Meanwhile, George was spending a long weekend with an old friend of his—she was in the shop just now, finishing her purchase. He said *purchase*—as opposed to her *order* or (even worse) her *shopping*—as a reminder, a little linguistic tap, that, wherever George was from, certainly no family had followed him; yet he smiled all the same. And wasn't this a strange place? It was either beautiful or desolate, neither could decide. They looked at the mountains. Doreen was fond of the place, Jack said. Even the village. She'd sent him here, as a matter of fact, for her favorite cigars. He held up a strangely dainty shopping bag and gestured two storefronts down. *Cigars*, George thought—another detail that felt lifelike. It never would've made it past the producers if he'd put it in a script. Old women don't smoke cigars, they'd say, and slash it out. Madeline, George offered—and here he used her real name because it seemed unwise not to—was just praising the local businesses, particularly Mr. Houghton's cheese shop. The selection was so sophisticated, had he ever stopped in? It reminded him, he lied, of Europe, of his youth.

"You say that as if you weren't still a handsome man," Jack said. For the first time, their little play failed, and a heat flushed up from Jack's collar into his neck. George knew he'd caught it, too, and looked down. The sidewalk was a spilled macaroni of discarded cigarettes and he hideously craved one, a gift for his nervous fingers and lonely lips. He reached for his case and offered one to Jack and they stood smoking together. The ocean was hidden by the storefronts across the street but they could hear it, or at least the passing cars that sounded enough like surf to be it. A tabloid rack outside Houghton's shop offered an exclusive front-page story: "Monsters in Famed *Death from Above!* Based on Real Government Experiments!" There were photographs to go with it, supposed proof that George's enormous radioactive spiders that breathed fire and burned cities were out there somewhere in the desert. The proof, George said, was like all the other proofs—grainy, blurry, its shadows mushed together into a single dark grey, with perhaps one arachnoid star like an occultist's asterisk hiding somewhere in the ink. They'd done the same with high-contrast close-ups of

Mojave lizards when *Godzilla, King of the Monsters!* had invaded theaters that spring. The things people wanted to believe.

"George, you make friends everywhere you go." Madeline stepped between them and plucked the cigarette from George's hand but only held it, her hand cocked to the side as she scanned Jack—shoes, belt, fingernails, haircut—to see where he belonged. The wind was gentle enough and the street sheltered enough for her to get what she wanted, that little curl of smoke parallel with her eyes.

"Madeline, this is Jack Turner. Jack, this is Madeline."

"Morrison."

"Madeline Morrison."

Jack kissed her hand. "I can't believe it," he said. "Even more beautiful in person than on the screen. I never would've thought our old George was such a jet-setter."

"*Jet-setter!*" She laughed. "Oh, that's so interesting. George, he's wonderful."

"Jack is rather charming, yes," George admitted.

"You must have dinner with us."

Jack blushed again and looked away. "Well, thank you, that would be more than a fan could ask for. I don't really want to bother—"

"You know I'm going to insist."

"Then I suppose we'll have dinner." He laughed. "George has my phone number. Perhaps you'll let me know—"

"Right now."

Jack froze.

"I do hope you haven't eaten," she went on, and touched him on the shoulder. "We were just about to throw together a little something, quite simple, a little wine and cheese and bread, but with all the best. I always insist, George knows, on the best."

"She is insistent," George agreed.

That color had drained back out of Jack's face, and taken a little extra with it. George felt helpless as Jack dragged deeply, as he
shrugged and exhaled into the sky. "Then we'll have dinner, won't
we?" Jack said. "You really are too kind. All the rumors—the good
ones, of course!—they really are true."

Madeline at last pulled from George's cigarette and handed
it back. "I apologize for the frantic, last-minute nature of the invite, but I do find that whatever we want most is best seized in the
moment. Besides, these really aren't things to overprepare for, are
they?" She smiled and touched, again, his shoulder, and waited patiently as Jack searched his pockets for something to write on—a
little leather notebook, say, embossed with the seal of the United
States, which lay hidden behind Jack's hand as he wrote, carefully,
the digits of Madeline's house number and, should he get lost (there
was only one road, George thought), how to reach her by telephone.

"We'll see you momentarily, Jack Turner," she said, and slipped
into the car. Alone again, George turned to him and made the face of
an apology—he hadn't meant for this to happen—and told Jack he'd
see him shortly, but to take his time, don't feel like you have to rush.
There was much, George thought as they drove away, to sweep under
the rugs, hide under the furniture, and stuff deep into the closet.

"The way he looks at you," Madeline said bitterly as she
watched for the first glimpse of the beach. "The stuff of love stories, George. All the best ones."

—————

Dinner was haunted but not catastrophic. In fact, George told me,
you'd think they were all normal people having a good time. Walt
and Madeline sat closer together and touched one another now and

then—on the arm, above the table, or more visibly surreptitious, on the knee, as if it were a secret. He lit her cigarettes and she laughed at his jokes. When she made to retrieve a shawl—the beach cooled quickly once the sun was down—Walt stood and helped her with her chair. They acted, effortlessly, as if they were in public.

Jacques, of course, did not belong—and he knew it. They chose to leave his presence unexplained. It was ridiculous to lie, to say he was some nephew or relation, but impossible to tell the truth. He said little. He laughed at jokes—especially Walt's. There was a constant twitch roving from here to there in his body, from his eyebrows to his fingertips. Mostly he stared at Jack when he thought Jack wasn't watching. George couldn't blame him; Jack was Hollywood handsome without its delicate deviations, if you could call them such—the mannerisms, the texture of the skin, the dexterity of the fingers. Jack was what Jacques would call, with a moan in the back of his throat, a man, and after being in his presence the boy would need, George knew, a great deal of attention. George hoped that Walt might drink too much to be up for the task and that Jacques would find his way to his own room; he was feeling amorous himself.

After dinner there was champagne, and after that a farce of dancing. It was cool on the patio, if not cold, which made it easy not only to stay clothed but to drink slowly, to sip only when there was nothing else to do with your hands. Madeline was seasoned at managing secrets, even if no one there believed anyone else's secrets. It was important, she would have believed, to at least acknowledge the decorum of it. Jack, after all—as George himself had noted—was not a boy or an older, married man; he was an equal, and that equality was threatening. There must be nothing direct, nothing concrete, and George was grateful that Madeline knew it. This wasn't, as it were, her first role.

"I'm so spoiled," she said, feigning the right amount of tipsiness. Jack led her in a gangly waltz around the pool while George and Jacques and Walt wallflowered along the balcony, the moon and its strewn splinters in the surf at their backs. It was honest, and George wondered how long it'd been since she'd taken a lover of her own rather than play chess—or checkers, rather—with the terribly, terribly interesting men she tended to collect. She was a lonely kind of spoiled.

Eventually they did drink too much. Jacques fell asleep on the divan in the salon, and Walt passed out in a lounger by the pool. Madeline covered him with a blanket and smoked with George and Jack as they split—she insisted—another bottle of champagne. Pickled as she was, she had nothing on two adult men in their prime, and her sentences, usually so elegant, crumbled into the mangled, shameful English she'd tried to leave behind in Missouri. Her vowels pooled as their sculpted ice began to melt and her face eased into something she'd never forgive them for remembering. She would be right back, she promised, she only had to visit the ladies room, and they didn't see her again.

"If I don't walk this off there's no tomorrow for me," Jack said. "How do we get to that beach?" As he gestured over the balcony, his glass slipped from his fingers and vanished without a sound into the brush below. Someday it'd be found, pummeled into a little gemstone. George imagined the archaeology of it, the narrative of lust they'd miss, whoever found it, in whatever new shape it made. George tossed his own over the rail and they laughed as it, too, disappeared from this earth.

It was a night made of paintings or the very best dreams. It was the way films used to be, how actors could walk along a beach at midnight and still smile, still yearn, still express themselves in whatever way their roles demanded with none of the murk of the real night. Jack must have thought the same. "They could make a hell of a sea monster flick here," he said. "It's lit up like a studio. And the beach never quits."

"It could rise up just there," George agreed, and waved his hand out over the water. "Perhaps from beneath a few sailboats, and head toward land. It could tower over the beach."

"Like a tidal wave."

"The beachgoers would scream and scatter. Sandcastles would be trampled, children separated from their parents, dogs barking in terror. A siren, as if the bomb had finally arrived."

"What would it want, George?"

He thought for a moment. It would depend on the monster, of course—something reptilian or humanoid would have desires, it could seek justice or revenge, whereas something more ancient, something tentacled and oily with ammonia, something with too many eyes, would destroy and eat indiscriminately, without stopping. "Nothing," he said. "It would want nothing."

Jack kept his eyes on the beach. In the moonlight his footprints cratered out white as the sand compressed beneath his bare feet. They'd left their shoes on the steps to Madeline's terrace.

"To want nothing would certainly make it a monster," Jack said.

The water teemed with stars and the hills had flattened themselves into backdrops. The cinema of it made George feel watched, as if he'd forgotten his lines. "I came out here to relax," he said, just to try the sound of it. "To unwind, as you say. I don't think I realized it, but the pressure—if you don't let it out . . ."

"I'd say it's awful, having a hit film," Jack said, "but I wouldn't know."

"Nonsense, Jack. All your films are hits."

Jack laughed and put his hand on George's back. It heated him through and he wanted to wear it there forever. "Sounds like you've seen a different balance sheet than the one they show me. The way Edwards looks at me, you'd think he was about to chain me to my desk and give me a bowl of dog food until I shit out a *Searchers* or a *Gone with the Wind*."

"Until you humiliate yourself, you mean."

"That's the whole game, George. If you don't debase yourself, how do you expect to buy a Cadillac?"

They must have walked for miles, George told me, and talked just as aimlessly, as leisurely. The sea would be full of migratory creatures. Jellyfish, Jack said, were known to sting here. There was always someone screaming in pain whenever the beaches were overrun—and rightly so, he added, since it felt like being branded with a hot iron. There were crabs scuttling down to the waves where they jettisoned their young, which didn't seem, George speculated, like a terribly smart way to ensure the survival of their species. Which human beings were perhaps least qualified to judge—the species that not only couldn't seem to ensure their own survival, but would in their inventiveness, their science, ensure the extinction of all others. Jack laughed but it suddenly shook him, George, how terribly sad it was to know that all of this, the burning jellyfish, the stupid crabs, the glittering sand, even the great pyroxenia of stars, would be nothing but ash and scorched, irradiated dust. It no longer seemed so ecstatic or purifying. It wasn't something to fear and drown in like a god. What it would be was total, a loss so unbearable that even the thought of it made him vomit onto the sand.

"Whoa there." Jack patted him on the back and gripped his shoulder. "It's never dignifying, is it? But always good to get it out. You'll feel better right away. Just take it slow."

It was humiliating to have so much heave out of him, not only his dinner and drinks but tears, sobs, tremors. Jack was patient and reassuring—"We've all been there, friend"—and never broke contact. By the time George had pulled himself together and they turned back, ready for another who knew how many miles, they were both quite sober.

"I always wondered if you were the emotional type," Jack said, and laughed to show George there was no judgment, no assertion of superiority or manliness. "My father was the same way and I never stopped loving him—well, once I got over hating him, anyhow. You know the phase." He clapped him on the back once more, less tenderly, and George wondered if something wasn't lost—left back there with his fluids in the sand.

Jack understood that George wanted some time off, he would cover for him at the studio—especially from the nosy little weasels like Ellman. George thanked him, he appreciated the favor and always respected those who honored his privacy, and Jack said it wasn't a problem at all. They arrived at the stairs and put on their shoes.

"Anyway," Jack said as they parted, "I'm proud that you're my friend. You're a beautiful soul. Try to make the most of what's left of the night." And he did. He hoped never to wake up again.

═══

The details in the morning paper were hallucinatory. Children, some as young as twelve, had taken up arms against the Soviets. The resistance fighters were nimble, disorganized, scattered—which made them difficult to find and suppress. They ambushed and immobilized Russian tanks. Budapest—which had left the war mostly unscathed—was, like many old capitals of Europe, a tangle of narrow alleys and dead ends, many of which were interrupted by staircases that made it impossible for heavy transports to follow them. The Russians, having left control of Hungary to its puppet government for a decade, knew nothing of the city, and they died because of it. Spirits, said the American reporters, were high. The people would never again, they said, wear Communism's chains. There was a renaissance of newspapers and dailies, some little more than a single broadsheet, that reported facts directly to the people, as well as opinions that had been suppressed for ten years. There were several strongholds in the city where rebels (so called) kept tanks and troops at bay, and where the fighting never seemed to stop.

Yet that very morning, George read, the Soviets had proposed a cease-fire. They'd announced this with the arrival of more troops—a show of force, it was said, just to remind the Hungarians that they didn't *need* a cease-fire, they didn't *need* to negotiate, it was only out of mercy. Many of the city's great avenues lay in ruins. Public buildings, armories, police stations, and storefronts had been shelled by the Russians; the Hungarians had torn the cobblestones to rubble to slow their movement. Cafés and markets were open. People waited in line for bread and for vegetables. The mood, the papers said, was exuberant. For the first time, George envied those he'd left behind.

He hadn't slept more than two or three hours but it didn't worry him; he felt invigorated, if a bit weak. His coffee and his breakfast were ready when he woke, and his desk, facing the beach where he and Jack had walked only hours before, lay like a spiritual feast. It would be an entire week of this, he realized—these silent, solitary mornings, this life Madeline had offered him as a gift. Everything taken care of. The old philosophers had been right to obsess over time and space; it was how a person stepped fully into their life—their inner life. Here was George and his great project. It was disorienting, he told me, to feel as if his life was suddenly worth something. Destruction is crucial in man's ethical development. It is reflective—as much a mirror as creation. To watch the objects, the accomplishments of man, shatter into their elements, is to watch the created world de-create. George skipped two lines and began again. Destruction is illuminating in man's ethical darkness. It lights the path—the same path we take toward creation. Look, after all, at objects. There was of course a specifically Communist attitude one was encouraged to assume when speaking of, or even thinking of, objects, but George did not share it. An object—or artifact, if we're to highlight its quality of artifice: that is, of having been made—was like language; it was a translation of imagination into a tangible or shared reality. What this meant was that human beings altered the world, and objects—like written language—were artifacts, visible artifacts, of that alteration. In them one could see the human will, which made them precious. They were imbued with love, no matter how unoriginal and cheap and ostensibly worthless. Which meant that the destruction of objects—including artifices like language or architecture or farmland—made visible the failure of the will. He pictured again the monster rising up out of the ocean and crushing the beach houses, the cafés; with its innumerable limbs it threw automobiles as if they were nothing, as if their engineering and craftsmanship did not and had never existed. In science fiction, George wrote, we relish our humiliation. He skipped two lines and began again. Destruction is illuminating in man's ethical darkness. It lights the path—

It wasn't even lunchtime when Madeline knocked gently and let herself in and sat in the lounge chair by the window. "Isn't it unseasonable today?" she croaked through her hidden hangover. "They say it'll surpass eighty degrees in Santa Monica."

George sat with his hands folded in his lap.

"I adore your friend Jack," she said.

"My colleague."

"Yes, he's so charming—and he adores you, too." She crossed her legs and sank deeper into the chair. Only yesterday, he'd sat there alone, reading for hours.

His day seemed over. He closed his notebook and pulled the page from the typewriter and lay it flat. "Jack and myself have been working together for quite some time," he said as he searched for his silver case. Madeline made no effort to provide a cigarette of her own. "We respect each other."

"Walt and I respect each other."

It wasn't the kind of lie George could challenge. "You know what I mean, of course."

"Yes, of course."

His case was beneath a leaning stack of books he'd pushed to the corner of the desk. The cigarette, he thought, was an artifact. Even rolled in some factory there was a tenderness here, an imagination of care; someone had thrown themselves against a world that couldn't have cared whether or not it contained such things, such pleasurable things. He exhaled and saw it, how his species had altered the world.

Madeline sighed. "I'm so lonely, George." Then she laughed and shifted forward in the chair, her wrists draped over her knee. "What I meant is that we'd never forgive ourselves if we didn't get out today. These late splashes of summer, they're such gifts. I've already called the boathouse, as well as Mr. Turner. We'll be ready to sail at noon, and we'll have our lunch on the deck. Oh, I can already feel it, can't you?"

He wasn't even sure, an hour later, that he felt it when they were on the real boat, this object of great luxury. Walt had bought it in the thirties, when actors and oilmen were the only rich people in the world, and cared for it neurotically. It brought him a great happiness. Even Jacques couldn't compete and stood helplessly next to George and then Jack and then George with his trembling glass of Vouvray. Likely he was still ashamed, George told me, from the minor panic he'd caused back at the house—even if it wasn't at all his fault.

"Those are your only shoes," Madeline had said as they were about to leave. Indeed, as George knew, they weren't just the only shoes Jacques had brought, but the only pair of shoes the boy owned. A sort of chukka boot that'd molted most of its suede, they'd come to look something like moccasins. She wasn't a militant, Madeline insisted—and God help her if she ever enforced the absurd rules of decorum of some people out east—but it was a matter, she said, of safety.

When Walt emerged from his bedroom, sweater and polo shorts and scarf and shoes and sunglasses all in place, he was surprised to find everyone in such spirits, not to mention Jacques hiding his tears by pretending to fish something out of his eye. Madeline sat on the bench in the foyer with her chin in her hands. George had retreated into a cigarette. Jack was to meet them at the boathouse and would now arrive before any of them, and George felt ashamed to associate with such people. "He's not at all prepared," Madeline sighed.

George looked at Jacques now as he held on to the gunwale. A navy sweater sat perfectly on his shoulders, and a pair of white shorts, George noticed, flattered him in a way that seemed almost insincere. And his shoes—a perfect, low-profile canvas with a navy trim. "This isn't the first time I've had to dress a young man for the sea," Walt had announced back at the house. In fact, George told me, the actor kept an entire closet, it seemed, for dressing underprepared and admittedly slender guests—for bringing them where they didn't belong. It was the kind of detail, he said, they'd never print in a man's biography, so I should enjoy this little gift of history.

"I still can't believe this," Jacques whispered in George's ear. "Even my dreams were never this good."

They anchored and had a late lunch about a mile offshore Anacapa Island, which rose and set east to west in the water like the crooked backbone of a killed whale. Its skin glittered like sequins as the breeze combed its curls of sagebrush and ceanothus. On deck, the staff had set the table. None of Madeline's guests had eaten oysters before, and she'd never looked so pleased. She lived for introductions, especially if they became lifelong loves. George was repulsed and delighted. Jack seemed to agree: "They're really not bad."

Jacques couldn't seem to slurp enough of their brine, their slither and salt. "This is the best day of my life," he said, and giggled as he put another shell to his lips and chased it with the wine.

The lighthouse didn't so much tower as peer over the rock, humiliated and purposeless in the daylight. A bump on the island's forehead. George watched it as Walt drew the anchor and sailed west and then south, into the channel between Anacapa and Santa Cruz, and lost it as they drifted into what seemed like the open and deadly ocean. It was a perfect day, inasmuch as what one's skin seemed to want of the weather. Even Madeline quietly enjoyed it.

Rarely, George thought, did it feel so good to exist, to do nothing but breathe. Likely it was stifling inland, where his apartment—he pictured it—is sitting unused, unventilated. Car exhaust dragging its feet through the streets. The landlady wondering, now, just when her European gentleman and his young friend will arrive from wherever it is they've gone. Palms dropping their fronds in exhaustion. A birdless afternoon of scorched flowers and dead bees and singed juniper needles. They are drinking, those who live in the city, not together but alone, nursing whatever they can as long as it's cradling a fresh block of ice.

"I don't mean to offend anyone," Jack said as he topped off their glasses, "but not even God could make a day like this." He tipped what was left directly into his mouth and gestured at the horizon with the empty bottle. "I wish I had more to say about it. But I'm also glad I don't, you understand me?"

The top three buttons of Jack's shirt were undone and his eyes carried the sea and the sun together, as in some ancient creation myth. George smiled. You must always know, he advised me all those years later, when there's nothing to say.

"It really is extraordinary," Madeline agreed. "And there's no offense here, not among us." With her glass she gestured at all of them, an atheist's benediction, even if she did linger, it seemed, on Jacques. Who knew what such boys believed, this day and age? "There are a lot of things, if you'll excuse the blasphemy, that God couldn't get quite right." She paused—you could always tell by the way her hands lingered in the air—but she did not continue and let go of whatever it was she'd wanted to add. She set her glass between her feet and pinned it against the deck. So it was time, George thought, to slow down—advice he took to heart.

The two Jacks didn't notice and opened another bottle. The

younger placed his hand on the elder's bicep as he steadied the glass. The shock of flesh shot through flesh. Anyone could see it. Before long, Jacques would do something terrible and incriminating, or simply fall overboard. George realized there were no illusions here; it'd been almost twenty-four hours since Madeline had wrenched Jack into this circle of deviants, and Jack doubtlessly knew what Jacques was for and to whom he currently belonged. No one provided him with a background, no one assigned him any use. In the movies, in all the stories, George realized, the lover he'd brought here was exactly the kind who got killed. Someone, he thought, had to be the first sacrifice.

"There we are," Walt said, and pointed into the distance. Another island had been born afore—as if it'd hissed up in viscous flames from the deep only then, bald and barren. "Speaking of God, this one's called Santa Barbara."

"They all used to be one island, you know," Madeline said.

Walt shook his head. "Don't pay any attention to that. The ones back there"—he nodded astern—"Cruz and Rosa and Anacapa, they all used to be one island. But this one's been alone for millions of years."

"I meant even before that," Madeline said. She took up her glass and knocked back a substantial gulp.

"Well of *course* before that. Everything was one island. It was all one goddamn island. The whole planet was just Australia, wasn't it?"

"This one isn't very green," George said. He stepped between them, as though it were an accident, and looked at neither—his gaze on the water. "I suppose because it's so isolated?"

"Pangaea," Jacques offered.

"Well," Walt began—his irritation vanished immediately. There was a story, as George intuited, behind its barrenness. In the previous century, Walt explained, as well as the early part of this one, the islands—all of them—were quite popular with farmers and ranchers; they offered, he said, a vast wealth of untouched pasture, a little piece of remote paradise. At some point, an enterprising young man had introduced rabbits from New Zealand onto Santa Barbara. This was only in 1942, mind you. Well, in no time—you know how rabbits are—there were thousands of them and they'd eaten everything in sight, gnawed the island bald as a man of eighty or a boy of ten. But that wasn't the end of it, Walt was saying as they sailed closer, no—just two years ago, he said, the National Park Service (all that damn Roosevelt money, sitting there doing nothing) initiated a rabbit extermination program. "They're trapping them," Walt said, "poisoning them with strychnine. Shooting them for sport, rounding them up and bludgeoning them. It's a regular holoc—a regular massacre."

George held the gunwale and looked for life on the island. They were still too far to see anything, though one might have assumed, at the very least, there would be birds. There were none.

"Soon there will be no more rabbits," Walt announced, as if his audience were stupid. "Who's ready for a dip?"

At some point—George hadn't noticed—Madeline had gone below deck, and was now resurfacing with a pitcher of iced tea. She poured Walt's first, a violation of etiquette you could tell, George said, ate away at her very soul, but everyone knew why. They thanked her, and clinked their glasses with hers as they relished this opportunity to sober up. George was grateful he wasn't alone on this boat in looking out not only for secrecy, but for decency.

They anchored a hundred or so yards from shore. "I hope you gentlemen don't mind if I excuse myself from the water," Madeline said. "I'm afraid I'd melt and never quite find the way I used to be. And anyway"—she pretended to fight a feigned yawn—"I need a little rejuvenation." They thanked her, she was so lovely, they were so grateful, they couldn't be happier to have her in their lives, and bid her a peaceful beauty rest—not, of course, that she needed it.

It'd been years since George had thrashed his limbs in the water, but he remembered how, and in fact was surprised at how much of his grace he'd retained. Though he'd lived in Los Angeles for several years, he'd never been in the Pacific. It surprised him, how much closer he'd felt to the water in New York, and how naïve he'd been, in those days, to think it would be American to get in the water and crawl back and forth along the waves. It was what they did, after all, in movies, and he was pleased at what it did for his shoulders and his waist, even his lungs. But the deeper he dug into Manhattan, the less time he spent in the water. The people he spent time with didn't understand—and told him so—why anyone would do something so exhausting, so pointless. You'll die of pneumonia, pronounced one painter in his comfortingly alien, displaced accent—*new-mon-ee-uh*. Here, a continent away, the water numbed him a way he'd never felt, and he wished, suddenly, that he'd never given it up.

Before long, he and Jack hauled themselves onto the rocks while Jacques and Walt raced one another, increasingly chaste as the alcohol burned to sugar in their blood. All wore suits—the new fashion that'd come out of the war, which resembled a plasticky pair of shorts. George hadn't bared his chest outside of the bedroom in years and he felt Jack's presence next to him like a watchful animal, a creature of death. Jack's body, of course, he knew quite well, but relished it all the same. How the mesas of his muscles clashed against the alluvia of his ribs and, if you were particularly vulnerable to daydreams or needful of metaphors, had something of a wind-confused desert in its windings, dunes in the dun of his chest hair.

"You know, George," he said, "we don't need a circus like this to get a drink now and then."

"Of course not. Less than a week ago we shared a drink at the studio."

Jack laughed. "Clever. You know I mean outside of that god-forsaken place. You know I mean as friends." He put his hands behind his head and closed his eyes and left himself unguarded. All that remained of their swim were drops on his belly, some saltwater pooled in his navel, and little tangles of the sea still clinging to the hair, the very dark hair, in his armpits. They were grown men, George reminded himself. Men, he recited, with reputations, with careers, with someone to call when it was time to sue for libel. Old enough for the skin, where the sun rarely touched it, to have lost its elasticity, its depth, and gone to wax. Jacques's body, for example, was not like theirs; he was taut as drumskin. No, if George smiled too hard or frowned too intensely, it would never quite come back, not exactly the way it was. But Jack made it look all right.

It was terrible to have never been a boy, George admitted. Not a child. Everyone, for a while, is a child. But to have been a boy. A youth. To have lain next to a peer like this at fourteen, at sixteen, or even at twenty, away at some college. To have not known better, not exactly, and to have faced few consequences even if they had known better. To have gotten up to no good, as some said. To have made a mistake here and there, or got ahead of himself. Several inches ahead of himself. (He wasn't about to brag, he told me—as if I didn't remember.)

But that hadn't been his life. Some go from childhood into

adulthood, even if one's voice hasn't quite caught up. And it wasn't even, per se, the war that had done it, or his country's aspirations. He'd simply lived in a place, in a time, where boys didn't exist, where instead there were millions of small, unfinished men who wore suit coats and carried valises, sat at cafés and desensitized themselves to coffee, to beer and cigarettes, until they liked it. Until it was, as they used to say, to their taste.

Undoubtedly Jack had been a boy. He had a happiness about him.

"Friends," George said.

Jack opened his eyes. "Tuesday," he said. "After I'm done at the office, I'll come out here, check in on Doreen, then swing by Caligula's palace over there. I think half past six oughta be right. We'll grab a drink and a snack and see the new Heston thing, that big biblical mess. Thou shalt take him seriously and so forth." He smiled at his own joke—something he could sneak into a script, if he wanted, since *The Ten Commandments* belonged to another studio. There weren't enough digs, as Jack called them, at other movies in this town. Wouldn't that be a hit, a movie that turned one of those big expensive gambles into a cheap little joke?

George was soaking up the sun; he wanted to remember everything he could about such a day. "It does sound delightful," he said, or sort of moaned.

Maybe they were wasting their time, Jack continued, on all these war and monster flicks. Maybe they should get into comedies. Maybe they should write—

A screaming interrupted them, unmistakably Jacques. They got to their feet but the sun had shifted and the afternoon water was a molten, searing gold. He was dying, George was sure of it. The moment had come.

Walt emerged from the water with Jacques flung over his

shoulder, like killed game. With every step Jacques gave another scream or groan, and sank into hysterics when Walt, as gently as possible, laid him back upon the rocks. The sting had lashed his abdomen, just beneath his navel, and was already rising into a welt. It wasn't anything to worry about—even George, a rube when it came to ocean life, could tell the boy would survive. But the pain was real, and from the sounds Jacques made George could scarcely understand this particular species of pain. The way he writhed and wrenched his limbs made it seem as though something alive and made of fire would burst out of his body at any moment. He filed that image away, a future monster.

"It's okay, it's okay, I know it hurts." Walt was holding his hand and petting the wet tangle of his locks. "You're fine, it's just a sting. Nobody's died from a jellyfish sting."

Which wasn't true, George told me, but such facts weren't worth getting into, considering the circumstances.

"Here," Jack said. "There's a way, but it's not exactly pretty."

"Anything," Jacques screamed.

"Take down his shorts." Jack waved, as if that were enough to make them disappear. "Just take them off, frankly, or they'll get ruined."

Walt blushed as they worked to untie and slide the boy's shorts away. George assumed his own skin, too, had gone hot. He saw that Jacques had spruced himself up, perhaps for Walt, perhaps simply because he wanted to. All his hair was gone, shaved bare. Even in excruciating pain there was shame on his face—and nothing quite cuts deeper, does it? They gently set his shorts aside while Jack got himself into position. "I'm sorry kid, but this should do the trick. I learned this in the South Pacific. If you want to close your eyes, I understand."

Nobody closed their eyes as Jack untied his shorts and brought it out in two wealthy tugs. The stream was quick to arrive and, to match the rest, rather abundant. He swept across the wound as slow and steady as he could and the rivers of it spilled down Jacques's pubis and thighs and coated his own penis, which, though hardening, seemed especially humiliating so freshly fished out of the cold ocean.

As Jack shook off the final drops, the boy turned to George. His eyes were bottomless. "Please, it still hurts."

George and Walt shared a glance and, luckily enough, were able to comply. They began together and hit him from either side, like a Roman fountain, as the boy's cock lurched upward with all the frenzy of his heartbeat.

Jack was tying his swimsuit when he came and stood next to George. He gestured down at the younger Jack, and even managed a little sneer. "It's always the little ones that have a mind of their own." He laughed as Jacques went completely red, as if his wound had taken over.

"Try not to spill anything else on it," Jack said.

═══

Another island. Docks here, and shelters, and a little harbor bobbing with boats. The heads of the palms and the crowns of the hilltops looked candied, as if dipped in caramel. Madeline seemed aggressively refreshed—George guessed she'd taken something—and the gentlemen she traveled with had rinsed and dried and dressed themselves for civilization. At the yacht club it was Madeline, not Walt, who asked for a table on the terrace that faced east. The city lay across the water and had begun its evening enchantments. It was best, Madeline whispered when Walt excused himself, not to mention the boat or the club or any specifics. "He's sensitive, as I'm sure you understand. No one likes to rely on his wife, especially when she's already so . . . so ancillary."

According to the club, it was Madeline's sailboat, and thus her membership. It wasn't something he'd ever noticed, George realized, but now that she'd said it—that Walt's mother was half Mexican—he knew he'd never be able to not see it. And he knew that she likely whispered behind his own back. *George—he's Jewish, you know.* It was the kind of currency a certain class of society, no matter who they voted for, still hadn't brought itself to liquidate.

"You know," she said later, as they cracked open their crab, "I dreamt of the most frightening screams, like someone being devoured."

The men said nothing.

"Honestly, you'd have thought someone was in terrible pain. It's hard to imagine such things just . . . just rise up from our unconscious minds, isn't that right?" She held a leg in her hand and gestured with it, another violation of manners, yet one she perhaps enjoyed, being the only one of them who could *really* belong in such a place. "Anyway," she said, "it reminded me of this wonderful party we all must attend. It's a Halloween gala, of sorts. A masquerade. On Wednesday. And no—you won't be able to tell me you have other plans."

On the voyage back to Malibu, in the last moments of sunset, something unimaginable moved beneath the water. It was alone and so much larger than the boat that no one could speak. It released a great breath, a plume of water almost thirty feet into the air, and sank. None of them had ever seen such a thing, and never would again.

Is any of this real? Could this possibly be the truth? Did such a day, I had to ask, really happen? Of course it did, George said. As inculcated, he began (in his accent it was a word that brought me great pleasure)—as inculcated as we are in the belief that we're meant for some great purpose, that tomorrow, he said, we'll live as the wealthy live, we are in truth conditioned to expect very little of our lives. It feels closed off to us to enjoy life. Yet we all have such days—at least once, but as often as not peppered throughout a life. These are the days we would see before we die, if it turns out to be true that we see anything at all. And the waves were there, George told me. The weather was, and the sun. At some point men had built, at Walt's order, a sailboat that many years later took them from island to island where they told each other strange stories and committed striking, unforgettable acts and ate food they would mention, decades later, as the bar, as the standard, that they'd never quite matched since.

Our beauty, George told me, was still with us. By then I'd heard my share of laments but it'd never quite struck me as unnervingly as it did then, how much it would hurt, when my own day arrived, to be thus abandoned.

No one had the energy, that night, to enjoy one another's company. Jack had a long drive ahead of him; Walt had passed out in the car on their way back from the boathouse and they'd decided to leave him; Jacques wanted to soak in the tub; no one knew where Madeline had gone. George, after a shower and a cigarette, sat in the chair by the window and held a book in his lap. He never opened it, and after ten or twenty minutes he undressed and went to bed. It was like a portal, he said, back to this planet.

In the morning he regained his privacy. His breakfast arrived on a tray with that day's paper. The Soviets had withdrawn; Nagy was negotiating with Moscow to establish an agreeable independence. So far, the Americans said, Hungary had shown no interest in appealing to the United Nations or to allying itself against Communism. Nagy urged the people of Hungary to protest peacefully. There was never any excuse for violence. They weren't, after all, animals but a people—a people who would soon be free. George clipped the article and shuffled it into his notes. Violence was easier to police than to suffer.

Reliably beautiful, a day in California. Another grain in the hourglass. When he needed it, the water was there to look at, and the sand, and if he stood close enough to the glass the bristly scalp of a looming cliff. Reliably, a species of numbness. Later he'd have lunch and coffee and still later a drink, some dinner, a conversation by the pool, another drink. It didn't seem possible that people anywhere were fighting for anything. George longed for a thought the way he longed for a cigarette—as something misplaced, something that sure would be nice. Instead, he pictured where he and Jack and this "circus" might go next, what beach or mountain they'd claim under their flag of leisure.

Around ten, he got a call from the studio. In the closet just off the foyer, where he could talk privately, he shut the door noiselessly behind him. "This is Mr. Curtis," he said, and heard a strange click before Edwards began his wheezing and rasping over the line. George glanced at the receiver but there was nothing to see, nothing unusual.

"Turner says you're out on vacation. Well, that's fine, Curtis, we take care of our own here. Every man deserves to put his feet up now and again. But I want to remind you that the business is movies, and the business of movies is money. One home run doesn't mean you can just wander off the field and do as you please. Now, of course that isn't what you're doing, and I'd never imply it, not for a second. I'm just calling to say you've got a good desk here with us, and I just wanted to remind you, and wish you a good period of rest. I can't wait to hear all about the next *Death from Above!* when you're back. What do you say? If we play our cards right, maybe we can finally take you out of black and white. Well, you're welcome and good luck. Call me anytime." George thanked him—not for anything in particular—and listened, in the silence, after Edwards was gone.

"Hello?" he tried, then hung up in case anyone might answer. In the mirror that hung on the back of the door, he saw his confusion. Why had he done nothing with his life? All these years and opportunities. He thought again of the monster on the beach, its ancient and alkaline greed that would pull them all under. FIRST, the posters would say, THERE WAS DEATH FROM ABOVE, BUT NOTHING COULD PREPARE THEM FOR . . . *DEATH FROM BELOW!* How many nightmares, George often asked me, came from some tired, ruined man standing in front of a mirror, watching the sadness swim across his face? How many of our great monsters were born from one unlived life?

Irrelevance was its own totalitarianism. It startled him to articulate it that way, and he went back to his room and wrote it down. But that was as far as he got, and he spent the day hovering over books and papers whose Englishes, Frenches, Germans, and Hungarians all untied themselves into loose, baggy strings of runes. In whatever war came tomorrow, America would win with a shrug. He left his room early and poured himself a sherry. There was nobody on the terrace and he drank alone, peering in through the windows now and then at a silent, empty salon.

It disturbed him, how lonely he'd become in only a day.

What George noticed:

Where the waves collapsed in on themselves and rolled frothily back into the ocean, a long, mottled strip neither water nor sand lay along the entire shore like a shed snakeskin.

Seagulls were unsure of themselves. The sky was full of aborted dives and altered courses and it asked for something close to pity, as one always pities the clumsy—even if we do laugh.

Stones had such history and such memories that we likely didn't even register in their vision, as frantic and short-lived as we tend to be. They wouldn't know we were here. This was perhaps what the writers of science fiction meant when they spoke of other dimensions.

A palm wasn't a tree at all. Each was a visitor and stood speechless, even embarrassed.

From the other side of the sliding doors, Madeline's furniture and décor were suddenly aristocratic. Even the tangle of clematis he'd watched the servants clip from the vine along the terrace that morning seemed, in its vase, lost to him.

There was a lonely depth in the lives of clouds. Miles and miles of them looking down upon another, never touching, even if, to us, they brushed past each other like subway commuters.

The ocean had no color. In fact nothing did. It was like all the paintings in New York—the longer one looked, the closer one came, the more each surface, each brushstroke, was a shatteredness of pigments. Life was this: a civilization of crawling, seething, single-celled tints and hues, a chemical metropolis of variegation.

It was frivolous to want anything of life.

It was obscene to ask for remembrance.

It wasn't a long walk, and with a single spasm of ocean water it would be finished.

As if it were an accident, he set his glass askew on the edge of the terrace and watched as it tumbled in a beige Pleiades of sherry. Again, no sound. He turned to go. Jacques was waiting on the other side of the glass and stepped out to join him.

"I thought you'd be at the cinema," George said. It was a Monday when they'd met, and Jacques had worked every Monday since. His own voice shocked him. He'd only been here, out on the balcony, for a few moments, but it'd been enough time to leave the earth—a traumatic place to return to. As secretly as he could he wiped the corner of each eye and said something he no longer remembered—that it was a beautiful day or that the ocean was so peaceful or that it hardly seemed real, this time they were having— but Jacques embraced him anyway. There were always people who knew and those who did not, and Jacques knew.

It'd only been four days, living at Madeline's, but lifetimes can be like that. Everything was different. They sat together at the table near the pool and appreciated each other's hands—a light touch, a squeeze, a trace, an unknotting, a stillness, a warmth. Jacques couldn't go back to the movie house. He'd sat around all morning and couldn't quite convince himself it was real, standing there taking tickets, thank you sir, enjoy the show ma'am. Putting on that ridiculous hat. It didn't matter what he did, he just couldn't do that. He couldn't pretend none of this had happened. It was such a young person's speech and George enjoyed its sincerity. He'd tasted real life, Jacques, and would chase it to the very end— and whatever else he said. They were tender together in a way they hadn't accessed until now. He touched Jacques under the chin and said, "How hard could it be, my baby cabbage, to steal someone's house? We could be very happy here." They would change the locks, they promised each other, and throw out all of Madeline's old clothes. They laughed as they imagined her scratching at the windows, shaking one of her stoles at them as if it were a dead cat. Nobody bothered them all evening.

Tuesday: he woke alone, he read, he looked through his notes and marginalia, he evaluated his *G. W. Kurtz* on the manuscript as though he'd simply chosen the wrong label, he looked out the window. He typed, *It's useful for me to believe my efforts are irrelevant*, and felt defeated. *Appeasement is its own species of destruction: But what have I seen?* Smoked another cigarette, had another coffee. At this rate he'd kill himself before he made it through the week. He went back to work.

At four o'clock, a young woman knocked apologetically and said he was wanted on the foyer telephone. It was Jack—a revelation. He spoke fast, reinvigorated by the studio's pace.

"I'm picking you up at six, George. Nothing fancy but bring a jacket just to have it. And because I know you, here's your warning: Don't even think about playing that 'Aww, shucks' or 'Jack, I wish I could' card on me. You're not under the weather, you don't have cholera or measles or the black death. But what you will have is a solid case of madness if you don't liberate yourself from that house, so six it is." George didn't even realize he was grinning until Jack heard it in his silence: "I know you're enjoying yourself," he added.

"Aww, shucks, Jack," George said. It sounded absurd in his voice, as if he were in one of those new movies full of Frenchmen and Italians masquerading as Americans. He laughed when Jack echoed it back to him—*Aww, shucks*—and hung up the phone. When he emerged into the foyer, he heard Walt shaking a martini in the salon. Jacques was there, and Mr. Houghton from the cheese shop. Madeline. She said nothing—didn't even look at him—as she reached out for his hand. He sat with her as she held it and listened to Houghton's story, some monologue involving a film and an island and a trained bear that kept stealing all the fruit. Walt placed a martini in his other hand, and George sipped as he watched without listening. This time in his life—as it was happening he knew he would always think of it, always look back on it.

At twenty to six he excused himself and went back to his room. The gin had done its work and he looked disinterestedly at his reflection, glazed as he shaved and rinsed and wet the one lock of hair that still draped over his deepening forehead. He put on a fresh shirt and, to his surprise, arranged a handkerchief in his jacket pocket as though its silk were blossoming. It was five to six. He sat in his chair and waited, thinking of all he hadn't done today, and how it was no longer so easy to care. There was his work—his life's work, if we're to use such a phrase, George told me, the way it's meant to be used. One has to laugh.

At precisely six he stood and walked to the salon. He made a show of it—thanking his hosts for their hospitality but he must decline this one night and regrettably had other plans. And before they could ask or offer or insist or interfere, he heard it: the double honk of Jack's Chrysler.

———

At a piano bar on Sunset—the kind you sank down into like a dugout or foxhole—they drank bourbon and laughed at poor Madeline, poor Walt. What ridiculous lives they'd created for themselves, right George? Poor rich people, you had to pity them.

They shared the elbow of the bar and from there could see most of the long, narrow room—from its booths to its doorway, open to the street above. It wasn't a walker's city but there were, gliding across the golden lace of sunlight and junipers, a few passersby whose shoes and boots suggested, George thought, a realm that would never pay them any attention, no matter how loud or how talented the pianist. Down here the drinkers were mostly men; it wasn't the kind of place anyone brought a wife or a date. George did not say this, but I'd like to make it clear that, in such environments, men like George feel fraudulent and anxious. They become imposters. It's not simply a matter of belonging or not belonging but of confronting what is supposed to be "authenticity" with an even greater degree of artifice; where everyone else in the room—at last able to *relax*, to *speak his mind*—sets down his mask, ours is made heavier. To be alone with men is, for men like us, the call to give the performance of a lifetime. And we are called far too often, if you want my opinion.

But Jack, too, was an imposter here, and, while he couldn't say it, George certainly knew it. Or he hoped it and called that knowledge. If one's ears can't help but hear, one's eyes can't help but say. It was them against everyone else, he imagined, and for the first time in a bar full of jazz and cigar smoke and the vilest jokes imaginable, George was relaxed; he could enjoy, he told me, his drink, his chat with an old and close friend.

So he drank perhaps more than he should've.

"She'll never admit it," he told Jack, "but Madeline was born without a personality. It's tragic but she manages, she gets along, as you say." He smiled at his own cleverness, pleased even before the analogy left his lips: "She resembles one of those birds who build everything out of refuse. A nest full of other people's things, their stolen jewelry and discarded keepsakes."

"But Georgie, she can't help it. She just finds you so *interesting*."

Georgie. So close he could almost hear his real name knocking around in Jack's throat. He leaned into the drunkenness in his smile, which wasn't as severe as he made it seem; he just wanted to be liked, to be enjoyed.

"Seems hard to believe all they do is drink and eat and go to parties," Jack said. "Well, and act, I suppose. In fact Walt especially seems to do a lot of acting. I imagine he and that—that kid that was with us, what was his name?"

"Jack."

"Hmmm?"

"No, his name is also Jack. We call him Jacques."

"Cousteau."

"Oui, comme ça." George saw the vulnerability—where, after all, did Jacques come from?—and he lifted his glass to hold open the thought, the space, until he found something innocuous to fill it. "Madeline"—he forced a laugh—"she says this all the time, 'I collect people.' As if we are just things? Things, Jack." His Madeline voice, a little higher and geographically ambiguous, as if he weren't sure if he were making fun of an American or a Brit, made him blush. He'd never used it in front of another person.

Jack signaled the bartender. "What kind of people?"

"Oh," George said. He was unprepared, grateful to earn a question from the one man whose questions were, right then, the most valuable in the world. The bourbon had coated his memories like spilled-on photographs and papers, and he thumbed frantically for something he could recognize, something not blurred into abstraction. "You know . . . collectible people, I suppose. Artists, actors and filmmakers, scientists, ex-convicts, émigrés, journalists, musicians, dancers, men who ride in boxcars . . . There's a farmer,

I believe. Once, a circus woman, I don't remember her affliction."
The bartender filled their glasses another two fingers and Jack
thanked him with a nod. George, with no lack of awkwardness,
held his glass until Jack realized he wanted to clink them again in
celebration. "Writers," he added. Clink. A trembling sip.

"What kind of scientists?"

Had there really been a scientist? Had he said *scientists*? He supposed he must have, George told me. There are regions of the brain
dark as forest gullies that send out warnings. He looked there. It
took all his concentration and the look of it must have resembled
pain. Jack touched his shoulder.

"It's all right, George. I guess I've just been paranoid since I
saw that car parked outside their beach house." He reached over
and moved George's glass out of the way like a captured chess
piece. There was a certainty in his hands; they never wondered
where they did and didn't belong, and George watched them with
awe. "Maybe it's time for a bite. Something to soak this up, hmm?"

As they gathered their coats and hats, Jack said, "It's strange,
about Ellman." George must have looked confused, because Jack
went on: "He disappeared the same time you did. I mean, you
didn't disappear. But he hasn't been to work these last two days.
Nobody knows where he is. Couldn't get him on the phone, either.
Not that anyone'll miss him, but a man loves a good puzzle. Anyway, watch your step. Here we go."

George remembered something Jack had said. "What car?" he
asked as they arrived in the street. "Someone at the beach house?"
But Jack didn't hear.

Palms, billboards, stoplights. Everywhere losing that color like
seaside rust as it flaked away into a deep, dark purple. They could've
eaten anywhere, George told me—a restaurant, a diner, a burger

stand, a Mexican food cart—he couldn't remember. Nor did he remember the opening of the movie, only fading into it somewhere
in the middle, Heston demanding the freedom of his people—the
Jews, George thought as he watched this profoundly un-Jewish
performance—but there was something even stranger. The film
played on the windshield, and he wondered if there weren't something else in that drink and that he was hallucinating it now, from
memory, as Jack drove him home. But they weren't moving.

He'd never, he explained to me, been to a drive-in movie, but
he had heard about them. It was maybe the most American thing
in America, that people drove out to these deserted stretches along
highways and parked their cars and asked for snacks and craned
their necks to watch a film they could see much better, and hear
much better, from the comfort of a cinema. It felt like watching
something happen here on earth through a telescope on another
planet. Shadows swept back and forth across the bottom of the
screen. In some cars, teenagers kissed furiously, their hands
clasped on one another's cheeks as if they didn't know, or were
too afraid, to let them travel elsewhere. Children ran up and down
the gravelly walkways between the cars, screaming over the dia-
logue and the music that rattled the little speaker on Jack's dash-
board. When there was a gust of wind, the screen bowed as if it
were breathing, and the film bulged with it—the actors shrinking
or expanding, the sets distorted as if they were underwater. *Cousteau*, he remembered then, and turned to see Jacques—no, Jack—
sitting there in the driver's seat. He had one hand on a Coke that he
held between his thighs, and the other, George only just noticed,
resting along the top of the seat. If it were to fall forward, George
realized, Jack would be embracing him. It was enough, with the
liquor and the atmosphere and the incredible solitude—they were

parked far, he noticed, from the other cars—for him to sweat, for his pulse to race.

"Hell of a thing, isn't it, George? Supposedly the most expensive film ever made."

And it was long. At two hours, there was an intermission; others left their cars to relieve themselves and seek out more beverages and snacks and stretch their legs. The less innocent stood and neatened their skirts and sweaters. Jack and George stayed put. It wasn't until the film began to roll again that George noticed how hot the human body was, how it radiated heat. Ellman had disappeared. What did that mean—to "disappear" in a country like this one? The car grew warmer and warmer yet neither of them cracked a window. Jack shucked off his jacket and loosened his tie. George did the same. Jack unbuttoned the top buttons of his shirt. This George did not do. The windows had fogged—including the windshield, which blurred and softened the garish film. Did Edwards know? Is that why he'd called? At some point Jack had finished his Coke and set the bottle on the floor, his legs spread wide. His hand still rested in his lap and—just as he'd done at the office in what seemed a lifetime ago, another planet ago—began to run his thumb along a great, magnificent length that slept not so soundly in the shadow of his thigh. Had Ellman really left, that day, for a meeting? On-screen there were screams and there was music and there were great melodramatic speeches but George saw none of it. When a man is in heat, he told me, there is only one commandment. It never quite does us any good, but right then it seems our only salvation. Jack took it out and George moaned at the sight of it, and from there the rules were broken. It really was a hell of a thing, George told me. The film, of course—however it ended.

"We shall be monsters," Madeline said. "Ghouls—truly ghastly. Everyone will be so thrilled."

She'd turned them into an entourage, and they fit neatly in the back of a limousine, forced to look at one another. It was the first time George had ever heard an adult speak of Halloween, and he still wasn't sure if by that word Madeline meant the holiday he'd seen on television and in neighborhoods full of children or something else. Jack sat across from him, next to Jacques and Walt, while Madeline played with George's hand and reminisced with Houghton, on her right, about how long it had been since either of them had seen Victoria—Victoria Munson. He felt sorry for all of them but Jack most of all; it was George's fault he was here, having to suffer these people and waste so much of his time. Yet he was grateful, too. It was never a bad thing, to let his eyes drink more of Jack—this bountiful well he never thought he'd tap. It was terrible to be so close and maintain their indifference and this, too—the tension of it, the torture of it—George loved. It hadn't even been twenty-four hours. His exhilaration was humiliating.

And it was alienating. On this earth there are people who care and those who do not and George, chemically in love, increasingly found himself aligned with people like Madeline, like Walt. In that morning's paper, he'd read how villagers just south of Budapest had stormed the local headquarters of the State Protection Authority and taken an immediate and long-simmering revenge upon their not-so-secret police. The men were mutilated, tortured, lynched, and burned in a celebratory atmosphere that George found difficult to condemn yet too horrified to accept. That same day, Hungary began releasing its political prisoners en masse—thousands of people who'd been sent to prison for ideas, for statements, for being related to the wrong person, or simply for convenience, including His Cantankerous Eminence, the Venerable Archbishop József Mindszenty, who offered to the long-dead monarchy the same support that'd earned him his sentence eight years prior. People were free. They would no longer be intimidated. They wrote and published their newspapers and showed the world they would not tolerate repressive regimes any longer.

For George, none of it was real. It felt like reading a forgettable novel, and not exactly a triumph of realism. What was real was the table where he worked—or said he worked. His cigarettes were real and the coffee the servants brought to him, the windowglass and his robe, and the chair where he read, carefully and at leisure, the thoughts and ideas of men he wanted to emulate, men whose voices his longed to join. Jack was real and their walk that long night on the beach, and the monster they dreamt up and its threat to civilization. The way two men could park a car and extract such intense pleasure from each other's bodies against nature—that was real. He felt hopeless—and that, too, it must be said, all real.

Madeline squeezed his hand. "Our first stop is a bit of a novelty, but quite necessary, as you'll see." She lit a cigarette and made as if to look outside but there was nothing to see; the windows were glazed with some translucence and the sunset had Midased the city. Nothing but depthless gold—a miserable fortune of it like you saw huddled under a dragon in the old picture books, on and on and on. It wasn't until they stopped that she could say, "Ahh, yes," and nod cheerfully at whatever was outside.

It was a monster of a building. Someone had taken one of the great stone Edwardians—they seemed to be in Los Feliz, George observed—and fused it with a modern cube, as though they'd teleported through time together and got mixed up on the way. How had no one stopped this? Why had no civic authority intervened? There were ornate rails of woodwork that slammed lifelessly into concrete and large, rectangular windows milling about like new, vacant money next to the staid aristocracy of stained glass. A petite balcony met an angular, expansive terrace where someone had placed antique garden furniture.

"Well then," Houghton said. At least George wasn't alone in his horror.

"A bit of a novelty," Madeline said again. She was so proud. While it didn't belong to her, certainly, it was another item in her collection and she was thrilled to see how it affected them. It was a great compliment to react, no matter how one reacted.

On the veranda—or what was left of it—a pair of ladies waited in the shadow, the darkness of it sharpened by the angle of the sun. It wasn't until they were approaching the steps that George saw they were the same woman twice over.

"Gentlemen," Madeline said, "this is Gretel and this is Gertie. They are sisters and this is their home." She did not introduce them, the men of her entourage, and the impression was that it wouldn't have mattered. Gretel and Gertie were polite but indifferent. It wasn't, George speculated, of any interest to them whether or not these visitors ever returned. Or perhaps they knew they wouldn't. Whereas they, these twins, would certainly be remembered, scarcely anyone visiting them—anyone but Madeline, whom they greeted by name—had a chance at being remembered.

If the house was a museum, they seemed to relish belonging to it, another oddity among its jarred and fish-eyed cadavers (bulging squirrels, George told me, and fetal pigs, and insects and arachnids, the bloated head of a goat, warped snakes and frogs), medical textbooks and journals in a whole continent of languages, instruments (specula, surgical lenses, prostheses), models of buildings and small replicas of cities, masks and wigs, chemicals (acetone, formaldehyde, enormous bags of titanium dioxide, borax and beeswax, talc, and others unpronounceable, George said, or at the very least unrememberable), wax body parts, photographs (actors, film sets, European alleyways, beaches, a striking number of desert landscapes in bloom, dead animals, the twins themselves), and film posters. George didn't know it at the time but the twins, in their late romanticism, had created what is now an influential aesthetic: the Hollywood fusion of Darwin and Mary Shelley. Ever after, when we watched some film together or perused the old biographies of makeup and effects artists, he reminded me of Gretel and Gertie, long dead, and that time they'd turned him into a vampire.

The film posters were a unique collection among Hollywood personnel, and as they finished his makeup he told them this. It wasn't often you saw so many studios side by side.

"We no longer work for any studio," said Gretel (he thought). "Everything we do is a singular project, one contract at a time."

"It's liberating," said Gertie (he assumed). There was something of an aggression in it, as if to reassure herself. George received the message and didn't say more. It wasn't polite to ask the blacklisted, however talented—however much their skills transcended their banishment—what had cost them their security.

"You even have one of mine," he said, and gestured at a poster for *Dr. Lightning vs. the Fire Planet*. It felt strange to acknowledge it, that he, too, worked on films that required makeup and creatures and false gore, and he regretted this weakness—an obsequious desperation.

But they smiled. "We are familiar with your work, Mr. Curtis.

When Miss Morrison told us you were to be our guest, we were quite pleased."

"Were you? That's so—"

"Please remain still."

When they were done, he looked the part. Had they known, somehow, where he was born? Had they translated his accent? Was he this obvious to everyone? The sisters had accentuated his cheekbones and the hollows around his eyes. His skin was pale despite its recent pleasures in the sun, and the tendons and veins in his neck highlighted with a bruisey blue. The fangs they'd inserted into his mouth—"Just pinch them with your fingertips, when the party is over"—further exoticized his unplaceable (he thought) European vowels and pushed his upper lip out into a royal overbite. He looked ready to corrupt youth.

Of Madeline, they'd made a terrifying witch; of Walt, her brooding warlock. Jack was a monster pieced together from corpses—given stitches, staples, and zones of flesh that varied in tone. Jacques was a little werewolf, less threatening than he was a startled, defensive dog. Houghton, buried under plastics, was some sort of fish creature, stuffed, as it were, to the gills with paint. Years later, George would wonder if it wasn't all those chemicals, a single evening as the Creature from the Black Lagoon, that gave him that fatal tumor.

George did not want to leave, but it wasn't up to him. It was time, Madeline said, for the party—which seemed to George uninteresting, expected, even bland compared to a house such as this, a living museum. Throughout their visit, the twins had been confined to their studio, preparing one costume after another, and there had been no opportunity to ask them about their collection, to hear the stories or the undoubtedly strange facts associated with each item. These were the kinds of people who deserved attention. Victoria Munson, he thought bitterly, had been a silent star for a reason.

They arrived at Miss Munson's home just after midnight. No one with any self-respect would arrive sooner, Madeline had said, not on Halloween.

It's long gone now—some kind of apartment building or grocery store took over its rolling expanse—but it was, George told me, one of the greats. A gatehouse, a canopy of elms as they climbed up the driveway, a cardinality of gardens each with its own mood, and the resting hulk of the house itself, a spider of Spanish turrets and breezeways and vaulted roofs. Even then it would have been forty years old, a monument to the earliest excesses of what all of them, these people, had moved out into this desert to do. In those days, George told me, the studios would've been just down the street. Every once in a while you'd drive by one of them, long ago turned into a brake shop or a common warehouse. It was sound, George explained, that took Hollywood out of Hollywood. Sound required space—not only for the equipment and the insulation but the distance between sets, and isolation from the city itself. Back then, George said, some car would arrive for Miss Munson and take her less than a mile for a few hours at the studio, where she need not even know her lines because there were none, not really. None of them had been prepared for that future, for something so seismic.

Like all ostentatious houses, its hulk spread outward from a central hall flanked by two great fireplaces. Both were carefully tended, and with an astonishing array of candles Miss Munson's party—restrooms aside—was entirely firelit. This was especially impressive, George told me, because in addition to waitstaff and musicians, Munson had hired dealers and game tables, whose

cards and roulettes and dice trembled with the drinks and cigarette smoke. So too were the masks and costumes brought to life
by the firelight, and George was conscious of how marvelously the
twins had done their job. He wasn't used to outdoing everyone at a
party. Madeline, of course, had known what she was doing. Everyone complimented them.

Victoria Munson, especially, was thrilled.

"I've never been so frightened in my life," she said, her voice
long genderless from cigarettes. Politely, she'd kept her costume
quite simple: cat ears and plastic whiskers, with a tail she wore
draped over her shoulder rather than dragging out behind her. It
wasn't a nice thing to notice, George told me, but she was strik-
ingly old. Not in a bent or gnarled or ruined way, nor wrinkled
and sunken, but in the way of stones—the stones, he remembered,
he'd observed on the beach back home. Back in Malibu, he meant.
She was a person who'd watched, who'd waited for an age, a great
center of stillness.

Someone in white gloves and a black mask handed George a
martini, and another to Jack, and another to Houghton. Another
person, dressed identically, served Madeline and Walt. Jacques
was offered nothing and no one knew how to address this, least of
all Jacques. He turned and watched a game of baccarat that no one
invited him to join. George drank half his glass in one pull. It was
desperate, but he didn't know what else he could do.

"I thought," Victoria began, and put her hand on Madeline's
shoulder, "I thought it's been so long since I'd visited Las Vegas—
why not bring Vegas to me?" Her laugh had something of a thirsty
motor in it and he saw the effort Madeline made not to wince.

At the word *Vegas*, Jack gave these two actresses his attention.
Neither of them noticed, and continued their little play as if George

were their only audience. Madeline smiled. "It's funny you should mention Vegas. Walt and I were just discussing another getaway for this weekend. In fact, we've already planned it—with something special at dawn. Can we count on you to be there?"

"Of course you can, my dear. Are these fine gentlemen invited as well?" Houghton had disappeared and Jacques was sulking and Walt was undoubtedly making a new, young friend somewhere in the dark. Victoria's gesture—her *fine gentlemen*—graced nobody but George and Jack, who had no time to object before Madeline's assent.

"Of course, there's no way to tear us apart these days. I'm so glad you'll join us. Nobody lights up the desert quite like you, Victoria."

George finished his drink and traded the glass for a full one. Jack wasn't terribly far behind him, swirling the last of his gin around an ignored, wrinkly olive. He snuck his hand into a shadow and touched George's elbow—shockingly intimate in that chaotic space. "What was that about?" he whispered as the two women moved closer to the fire—to backhand one another's careers, no doubt.

"I've honestly no idea. I've never been to Vegas and never intended to change that."

"What happens at dawn in Vegas?"

"Don't interrogate me, Jack." George was surprised and softened his face—which must have looked ridiculous with his bloodsucking features. In the dark, he touched Jack's chest, where a tattered vest hid the muscles George had marveled over—even worshipped, he was ashamed to tell me—the night before. "I'm sorry, I'm very tired. This gathering is perhaps more than I can handle at the moment." He sipped from his second drink, which seemed to him remarkably, almost impossibly good—a diamond of heat in his chest that brought a great, stupid smile to his face.

"Or perhaps in a moment all will be quite splendid. You never know how these things go, do you, Jack?"

They went, George admitted, straight to hell. It'd been years since he'd embarrassed himself with drink and whenever he thought of it after, the things he'd said and the people he'd insulted, he grew so ashamed that he considered—briefly—never again touching a drop. But it was also, he said with a note of pleasure, a delight to be a terror, a storm upon that ignorant calm. Perhaps this is what Madeline wanted when she encouraged him to be interesting—a foreign, even monstrous spectacle other people would gasp at in pleasure and chatter about later, in awe of the people Madeline knew.

But what was most wonderful was to take a break, even for a few hours, from his life being his own fault.

If it were a real casino, Jack told him later, George would've been shot. It began when he stood behind the players and read their cards aloud—"Ah, yes, the queen of hearts and four of diamonds"—giggling when they became incensed and shooed him away. He abandoned cigarettes in the drinks of people who said unbearably naïve things—or simply those he didn't like the look of—and stealthily (he thought) switched the hats of men and women sitting close together. The hired men seemed to have been trained not to intervene; even when George scooped up a pair of thrown dice from the craps table and plunked them in a man's martini, they simply produced another set and threw again. He was having such a fine time, he assured anyone who bothered to listen. One of the servants had been directed, he guessed, to follow him around, and he slowed their chase by blowing out candles, one by one, as they relit them in a hurry.

Nor was he the only misbehaved guest. Jacques, despite his

shunning, had found a way to get drunk and was crawling on his hands and knees, howling whenever a man crossed his path. A woman George had never seen before, dressed as some evil sort of nurse, was stealing plates of hors d'oeuvres from the waitstaff and offering them to other partygoers, but withdrawing the plate at the last moment, cackling as she deprived them of their choice. Victoria herself, even, seemed to have a unique habit of asking how you were enjoying the martini, and then plucking it from your hand and knocking it back. It brought her a joy George was grateful she could still experience, and he mused, in his drunkenness, that he'd have to get to know her better, to ease into her life as he'd eased into Madeline's and see what he could extract from it. It was the first time, George told me, that he admitted to himself how much he enjoyed using the rich.

"George, you must calm down," Madeline said as he came to switch her witch's hat with Victoria's cat ears. The two of them were on the settee near one of the fireplaces and were whispering about some great gift, a rare opportunity that Madeline was happy to share, that Victoria was the first person she thought of, the one who'd enjoy it most, and Madeline was so kind to always think of her, they must really see one another more often. Their speech was remarkably underslurred given how much they'd had to drink. Then he saw, for the first time, Madeline's secret.

"These are so wonderful," Victoria said as they each swallowed a pill. "Have you ever taken Dexedrine, Mr. Curtis?" She plucked the bottle from Madeline's hand and shook a tablet into George's own palm, which he was surprised to find waiting for it. With a little swallow of gin, it slipped inside his body.

Later, Madeline whispered to him as they waited in parallel lines for the restroom. "I was hesitant to suggest it, but I think you'll enjoy them." She slipped a little bundle of cloth into his pocket. "Another writer I knew swore by them. They helped him concentrate on his work, and once he stayed up for a fortnight straight and wrote a whole play. It won all the awards. Someday we'll take these like vitamins and our society will be unrecognizable—a race of super people who don't even need to sleep." He was sweating and his pulse was racing but he felt powerful. Everything in the room was something he could study and examine; every conversation around him registered in his brain. The dizzying effect of the alcohol was stabilizing and in its place he felt like a watchtower of intellect and reason.

"You absolutely won't sleep tonight," she said, and kissed him on the cheek before slipping into the water closet.

Of course George had known about amphetamines since his days in New York, when the painters and writers in his circle—was it his circle, or simply an orbit he'd transversed like an orphaned planet?—had traded them like cigarettes. Despite the occasional temptation, he'd never felt overwhelmed by the appeal, and didn't like how it gave one's teeth nothing to do but bite, bite, bite in frustration, in boredom. Reading magazines and listening to records and smoking cigarettes in a crumbling loft wasn't the same when all he could focus on was the clucking of a frantic jaw across the room. But, he told me, how he'd been wrong! It was the beginning, he said, of a long and rather arduous love affair. There was so much he'd never have been able to do without them. They came at a strange time in my life, he said, but they hung around long enough to make a difference.

At dawn, the servants dampened the fire and snuffed out the candles. The entire room was suddenly a smog of wax and cigarettes and body odor and sticky, spilled drinks, and no one wanted anything more to do with it. Jacques had stripped to the waist and was unconscious on one of the baccarat tables, the lash on his abdomen finally fading into a pink that matched his nipples, which gave George a stirring. Walt had vanished—one could only imagine with whom. Victoria was snacking off a fresh plate on the same settee as before, her tail coiled neatly in her lap. Jack was startlingly sober, if exhausted; his eyes looked as if they'd gotten too hot and had lost a little of their shape. Madeline offered him a Dexedrine, which he took happily. "It'll get you through the day," she said, and it was only then that George realized it was Thursday, the first of November—a day when normal people, which Jack ostensibly was, went to work. He imagined the empty office, George's desk undisturbed, Ellman's perhaps emptied, maybe even ransacked, his scripts and scraps cataloged and labeled and sealed away in a drawerful of evidence. Had he at last crossed a line? Had they finally put Ellman on the list?

Houghton was waiting for them outside, smoking and enjoying the fresh flowers. He'd lost his fish head and was a ridiculous chimera. "Like something straight out of *Gatsby*," he said, pointing inside at the remains of the party, but no one else had read it. They dumped Jacques in the trunk of Madeline's limousine as if they'd killed him, and Madeline disappeared for a half hour to look for Walt. Jack said he'd catch a cab to his apartment, where he had to wash this party off his skin. Already he was more awake, a boiling kettle hissing with ideas on his way to finish a whole movie in one sitting, George imagined. At one point, not long before they drove back to Malibu, Houghton suggested that they check whether or not Jacques was still alive, which he was—and so peacefully beautiful, so handsome, so young, and so enticing that George wanted him in his own room when they returned, any other man be damned. *Wanna see it again, mister?*—such lips, such a throat. Such, George thought in a sudden flush of heat, a rounded pair of cheeks under that suit, and such a taut and tender hole between them, like it was made, he thought, by the lascivious hand of God himself for wrapping its pink little lips around cocks like George's and milking them dry, every quicksilver drop. It was time, he thought, to live up to his costume and drain this werewolf of life.

"Say"—Houghton turned to him—"I'm sorry, George, but I've just remembered. Did that man ever find you? He must have been a great fan, terribly enthusiastic and interested. He knew all about you but seemed afraid to intrude." He lit a fresh cigarette and ground its predecessor beneath the webbing connecting his toes. Whenever drugs are involved, George said, you can never be sure what's real and what's chemical, but his heart was alive right then and panicked; he had all the certainty of a paranoiac, connecting one mystery to another. There was even a car parked just down the driveway, its windows dark, a lone orange glow from a single cigarette as whoever it was watched them. Jack had never described the car but George was sure that this was it, this was the one. "I should have said something sooner," Houghton said. "Did he ever introduce himself? He couldn't wait to meet you."

—————

In my final comments about George's life before he left, with his new friends, for that long irreversible night in Las Vegas, I'd like to point out that history is not for everyone. Or perhaps it's better to say that not everyone is for history, which is at best selectively amnesiac and, at worst, exclusive as Madeline's yacht club. These people and their lives, their accomplishments, are not written about elsewhere because they are not the kind of people it is convenient for history—that is, by *history*, the conscious efforts of organizations, governments, and institutions with a politics of their own, however objective they claim to be, however unbiased—to record or remember. They are not, in a word, winners. And because they lost, it is their lives that are—or nearly were—lost to us.

Madeline was right. George did not sleep, and instead began to work again, to seriously work. He gathered in his centrifuge a cyclone of starts and stops, observations, middles, conclusions, footnotes, asides, and counterpoints, and sometimes sat for hours with a pair of scissors and a pen, rearranging and refining his ideas until each clipped paragraph was an impermeable gem, and together they formed a crown. He asked the servants to bring him every newspaper and weekly they could find and he never stopped reading. Even after his workday had supposedly ended and he joined Walt and Madeline and Jacques on the terrace, his work continued as he shuffled through papers and notes he'd brought out with him. There was no longer any point in being private, in being discreet; he'd found a way to say what he wanted to say and there was no way anyone could refute it. He'd already disappeared twice in this life. There was no reason to think he couldn't do it again.

Besides, it was beginning to look as if the events in Budapest—which had, in newspapers that once used the word *rebellion*, been recast into *the insurrection*—were nearing their ugly end and would become an example or a warning in his work, rather than a hope. Here was not a transformation but a failure. Despite its promises of peace and accord, the Soviet Union had, in the early hours of that very morning, sent enough troops and tanks across the Hungarian border to exterminate every last living soul in the country George once called home. They surrounded the airports and checkpoints and train stations; no more needed to be said. In fact, George told me, nobody was sure, in those days, if anything more *would* be said, not with the Suez crisis suddenly banishing any talk of Budapest—if not off the front page, at least below the fold. Their emergency, their courage, was no longer stimulating to American readers. Even the United Nations had postponed "the question" of Hungary, which made every allied effort to foment and encourage the rebellion—including the embarrassing Radio Free Europe broadcasts that dangled Western civilization like a carrot on a stick—seem not only cowardly but malicious, sadistic. His people, George told me, had been abandoned. Yes, he still thought of them as his people; even now, to this day, they were his people. Betrayed, he told me, was not too strong a word.

It was then that Jack joined them—no longer a party guest, but a part of the amorphous commune Madeline had created with George's writing residency—and George began to imagine a different form of happiness. "Enough with pretense, gentlemen," she said as they dined that evening—she and George and Jack, and Walt, and Jacques. Their backdrop, as ever, was the sunset and the beach and the littlest mountains, the earliest stars; and George wondered— even as he waited for her to explain, to continue—how long a life like this could last with nothing to back it up, none of their Hollywood money, none of their security, their immortality. It wasn't long at all, as it turned out, but how could he have known on an evening like that? "And by pretense," she continued, "I of course mean your love for one another—or *feelings*, if we must tiptoe around such catastrophic words. Please cease this sneaking around, this awful game, and share a bed like the two grown men you are."

George felt himself go pale. He was sure that Jack would sue her for slander, that Walt would never work again, that their passports would be seized. Yet he laughed, Jack, and raised his glass to the man next to him. "They say you can never hide from a witch, right George?"

Madeline smiled and raised her own glass to hijack his toast. "To witches," she said, "and everything we know about you." She gave Jack a wink and took a long, luxurious sip. "I'd just rather everyone live their life out in the open, Mr. Turner. You understand."

There was no rendezvous at the beach, and no pretense of seeing a film. In George's room they undressed each other and took their time. It'd been years since George had accommodated a man and Jack was a lot to accommodate but he took it slowly and was deeply proud of what he accomplished. It was astonishing how the human body could metamorphose, could dilate and contract, could take within itself against any supposed god's design a substantial, precious flesh and hold it there in a unique, unparalleled pleasure that relatively few men on earth gave themselves a chance to experience. He turned and looked at Jack's face as they rocked against each other. He wanted this every day. He wanted this cock inside him at every moment.

"It's been haunting me, George, how you said the monster would want nothing. You remember? The beach? I think it would really get under America's skin."

George's hand was traveling over Jack's chest, this landscape he'd studied for so long and never thought he'd visit. "*Death from Below*," he offered.

"Have you ever thought about working together? I could help you with that sequel Edwards keeps mumbling about. That way, you'll have a reason to stick around once you're bored with me. I'm seeing it happen slow, people disappearing one by one, then whole ships, and then it comes for the town itself."

"It's more than that, Jack. It isn't just the water, it's whatever lives beneath us. Whatever's down there sleeping that we've woken. No one would be safe. It could swallow everything. It could pull us all down."

"Sometimes you give me the creeps. You've got a psychopath's mind."

George grinned and said, "I'm as harmless as a cephalopod, Jack." He plucked one of the hairs from his chest and laughed as he yelped.

At some point near midnight Jack fell asleep and bumped into him and got tangled and sweaty and restless. George lay there and thought. He smoked a cigarette in bed. He considered what had happened, what had changed. Then, in the morning light, he saw Jack's cock waiting like a sated creature asleep in the hot sun and gave it a bath with his tongue until it stood upright. Jack's hands were traveling through his thinning hair and pushed, gently at first and ever more forcefully, as George slowly opened his throat, and Jack bottomed out—sunk to the hilt, as they sometimes say. George felt Jack's heartbeat against his lips, at least until there was another pulse that drowned it out, and which George dutifully swallowed. He smiled in pride.

"I'm starting to appreciate your feminine side, George."

"I prefer to think of it as my masculine side." He wiped his mouth with the back of his hand and licked what was there, a cat's bath in reverse. "The other masculine side."

"Suit yourself, as long as you can do that again when I'm done at the studio. It's Friday—a man loves a good treat."

"One man's treat is another man's treat, too, Jack." He reached over and plucked one of the Dexedrines Madeline had given him from the little pile by the bed. "Now leave me alone."

If these are intimate details that bulge or drip from the fabric of the story I've chosen to tell you, I hope—as I'm sure George would have hoped—that you consider them not as queasy excesses or dilated indulgences but as acts of precision. In grief, one is handed the opportunity, wanted or not, to meditate on happiness, on where joy falls in time. No matter who we are, we spend much if not most of our lives pretending, and to pretend—even about something as mundane as fluids and membranes and the chemicals they call to, the brain cells ready to receive their good news—is not a path to happiness. We are happy with facts, and if it was a fact that Jack's motor neurons and muscle fibers were beginning to communicate in a pattern of chemically accelerating contractions, and the bulbocavernosus at the root of him began to tremble as the period between these contractions rapidly deteriorated, and the pearlescent, plasmic cocktail of fructose, citrate, amino acids, flavins, phosphorylcholine, dihydrotestosterone, zinc, and vitamin C—shaken as it traveled from gland to gonad to tip to tongue—shot out of his body with the familiar farewell of an oxytocic stupor, and if George, with the sophisticated discretion of his thousands of gustatory papillae, could relish this sweet-bitter, salt-tart gift, I would prefer it not forgotten. Too much happiness, especially a happiness like theirs, is forgotten. It dies with a man like George, and I don't know that anyone needs a reminder of a different sort of fact—that a lot of men like George did die, long before their time.

When his coffee arrived, George's mind had already cleared and uncoiled and was reaching its great tendrils into everything that interested him, everything that obsessed him. It was remarkable, not to feel exhaustion—the enemy of ambition. He would be able to work like this once he left—once he packed up his things and

returned to his apartment, apologized to his landlady ("Family,"
he would say, as if he had one), and resumed his work at the studio.
It would be possible, George realized, to get up early or stay up late,
to write his screenplays, collect his pay, go home and transform the
world—or at least resist, as much as one could, its transformation
into ash. Surely Madeline would keep him well stocked. Alive and
electric, George felt more interesting than he'd ever planned to be.

When Jack arrived, it was nearly six. George's forearms ached
from typing. He wasn't even sure what he'd written but he knew it
was something to work with, something to pare down. The more
there was to sharpen, the sharper it could get—at least that's what
he reasoned. Even if it was nothing, even if he had to start over, he
had at least created something. And here was its bulky evidence.
He stood up and met Jack in the salon.

Walt was already shaking the martinis. Since Madeline had
put an end to secrecy—or one species of it—their evening dynamic, as a little commune, had changed. Walt spent most of his
time, at home, naked to the waist, dressing only for dinner and
undressing the moment it was over. He did this for Jacques, who
seemed taken with his new, outward role as Walt's special servant.
They'd found a little Roman loincloth—something long stolen
from a period movie—and he wore it around the mansion and its
grounds like a uniform. He was careful to sit politely so as not to
offend (Madeline's word) the genuine servants, the paid servants.
George wished he found the whole thing obscene or embarrassing
but it tickled the reptilian part of his brain that said *look*, that said
want, that said *have* and *take*.

Jack, sitting there with his drink, seemed to take a different
pleasure in the boy's servile presence. Jacques was afraid to meet
his eye.

Madeline began. "You're very fortunate, George." Was he? "Quite—you see, Victoria is amused by disorder, and quite liked your little performance." It wasn't precisely a performance, and to be fair he *did* have regrets. "Well, she's a unique woman. Otherwise I fear she wouldn't have agreed to join us tomorrow." Tomorrow? "Yes, you see, after Halloween comes the Day of the Dead, which I've decided we should celebrate—another movement, shall we say, in our little symphony. It's so much more interesting, anyway, than any old Halloween party." Another party? Here? "Of course not. I have a room in Las Vegas for times like these. No one will be disappointed." She sipped from her drink and surveyed the room. It may have been simply because he was last in a chain, but her eyes landed on Jack. "I should also add that no one here is exempt. You *will* be leaving with us. Tomorrow. Just after lunch." It did sound rather intriguing. "Intriguing, George"—she laughed—"we'll all have the most wonderful time. You'll never forget it. Nobody will."

What was a party, anyway? This George did not ask—not of Madeline. But he did wonder. Wasn't this—drinking martinis and sharing conversation, listening to music, losing themselves in each other's company, stealing moments of intimacy when they thought no one else was looking, Jack's lips on George's neck, Walt's hand lovingly, menacingly resting against Jacques's throat as he asked him a question, lighting each other's cigarettes, going out to look at the stars, stripping down to nothing and splashing in the water, opening another bottle, forgetting who you were, that you *were* at all—wasn't this what people meant when they said "party"—when they said "celebration"? For George it was celebration enough, he told me—to be grateful together, and grateful for their lives.

When they said good night, he and Jack tried but could not make love, not at least in the way they were used to. Instead, sleepy with drink, they nuzzled like chilled cats. Here was another's skin, another's map of scars and secrets. Here was his scent and his softness, his neck's slow slap of blood. Here were his testicles. Here was the scar where they'd taken his foreskin, one in ancient ritual and one because, isn't it strange, it's just what people do here, nobody knows why. And here is the older scar, from glans to perineum, where before he was born he went from female to male. A little chromosome, they said, was all it took to sew it shut.

Jack slept like he was a boy again—mouth open, hands twitching, a little groan as something trespassed his dreams. In the moonlight George smoked his cigarettes and watched the man next to him and followed his thoughts. He couldn't remember when he'd last slept, but what good was sleep when you had this? I no longer remember, he told me, what it was I thought. That wasn't the point.

In the morning they packed like a family. Madeline called to Walt to not forget his pocket square, and Jacques asked George if he could borrow something to read—he hated long car rides and no one ever wanted to talk to him. It struck him, then, the profound pity he felt. Would it really have been so bad, George wondered, if Jacques had met another man, a simpler man, outside that movie theater? If he had been some other man's wife, and maybe even made him happy?

As they were waiting for the car, George searched his pockets for his cigarettes. He'd left them, he realized, on his desk—typing a few pages in a fury while Jack showered in the next room. When he went to retrieve them, Jack was there, too, his back to the door. He did not look up. George's papers were in disarray. His notebooks had been opened and set back in an unfamiliar manner. George was a neat, orderly person, and Jack was always rough, always just enough of a mess to charm you. Which, unfortunately for Jack,

didn't make you a very good informant. A spy, George said. Someone who lied to others in order to get what they want. Someone
who made others believe in trust, in companionship. Judging by
his frustration, whatever it was that Jack was looking for, he hadn't
yet found it. George slipped out of the room.

Among their busy morning, nobody had disturbed the paper,
which lay folded on the foyer table, just beneath the fresh flowers. George's hands were trembling as he wrenched and shuffled
his way through it in the back of the car—from rage or from fear
he couldn't say, which usually means, George told me, that it's no
insubstantial slice of each. And anyway, you can't have what people call *betrayal* without both. But it was wholly fear—without a
doubt, George said—when he saw, in a lurid little column a few
sheets in, that the body of Francis J. Ellman, missing since Monday
morning, had "been found." Another photograph, far crisper and
more credible than the radioactive experiments had unwittingly
given the tabloids: a familiar old coupe, battered with age, parked
along a monstrous pier in Long Beach, a familiar shadow slumped
inside. The newsman had already decided: suicide, cut and dry.

When Jack joined him, he handed over the silver case. "You left
these," he said.

"Thank you," George said. He extracted one and lit it. If you
breathe, he told me—if you tell yourself, *I am breathing*—you can
remain still, you can keep your latticed frenzy of muscle tissue
and nerves under control. He exhaled slowly, evenly. *I am exhaling.*
"Was there anything else?"

"Not that I could find." Jack turned and looked George in the
eye and smiled. "Everything we want is right here."

New York

SUCH TALK, ALWAYS, WITH SUCH PEOPLE. PLANS AND
ideas. Visions. Sentences of theirs are conjugated in the future—
the revolution *will*, the people of society *are going to*. No one is
faultless, of course. But it was better, George realized, to associate
with optimists, with people who not only believed in the good of
the future but believed it was they, in their learning and their ambition, who could reach it. Who could bring it into the present.
They are the opposite of those who go around mumbling about the
animality of man, about *human nature*. It was human nature, they
said, that unleashed the Nazi horror. It was human nature that
selected toward slavery, that raped and tortured. Whenever a man
starts talking about human nature, George said, you can assume
he means his own nature, his own inner life. No—you want to
follow someone who knows where they are going, and who wants,
with great love, to go there. Utopia is not a state; it is a compass.

========

George was born, he told everyone, in a movie theater. What he rarely said was that, for such a birth to happen, György Kertész had to arrive in New York. He was sixteen and it was summertime. His parents would be along shortly, they had assured him—it was just important that he get a head start, that he get the lay of the land, that he at last practice, they said, his beautiful English. It was 1944.

In his imagination, New York had been a city without a past. Which he hadn't realized, until he stepped into it, that he'd meant in his childish brain a city without a stench, without a punishing grip on the body. Never had he felt anything as sweltering, this carcinogenic swamp that smelled of lead and farty garbage, cigarette smoke, sweating onions and splattered oil. Instead of leaving his body in Budapest, György seemed to have sunk deeper into it, and lay naked on his cot whenever his landlady was out, an old Hungarian who'd left before the Regency takeover just after the first great war—a name and address his parents had folded among his most important papers. Every morning he washed and every evening he smelled like a creature that lived in a barn, and washed again. The new environment seemed to have awakened the man dormant in his boy's body and, among other problems, he gained nearly a foot in height—and so quickly that it left stretchmarks on his back. None of his clothes were any good to him and he spent his first earnings on new trousers and shirts. He'd found work at the shipyard in Brooklyn—a short train ride from his room on Clinton Street when he had a little money, and a long, drenching, humiliatingly human walk when he didn't.

Magda, who spoke of New York as a paradise even though she lived in relative poverty and fought with all her neighbors, kept him fed but he remained hungry. She talked with him but he was still lonely. On Sundays, she dressed him in her son's left-behind suits and took him to Madison Avenue, to Central Park, all the way out to Coney Island, but he continued to believe he'd made a grave error. If America was department stores and duck ponds and Ferris wheels, he didn't want it—only to go home. It wasn't, he told me, until later that he would find the bookstores and museums and galleries, the cafés, the apartments and lofts where people had their visions, the select inventory of public men's rooms, and, of course, the movie houses. In the beginning, he simply worked and spoke about the weather and waited for a wire, a telegram, any word at all of when his family would arrive.

They had come from Pest, a town house all to themselves not far from the Károlyi Garden. Even as a young child—the hand-holding age—György was such a creature of cities, of streetcars and cobblestone and wrought iron, that the garden continually surprised him. It was astonishing to see living animals—sparrows and finches, his mother said as he pointed, warblers and thrush. There were squirrels and even a rabbit, and there was nothing between them, these creatures and György, but empty distance, a stretch of lawn or an overhanging branch. It was nothing like the zoological gardens where animals, however impressive or terrifying, were cataloged, labeled—separated just as those in his books were isolated each on its own page. In the garden by his parents' home, a rabbit lived a rabbit's life. Later, he began to notice the bees and butterflies in the same register, nothing at all like the specimens pinned under glass in his father's study—murder as a pastime, György thought, stealing the lives of butterflies the way György painted watercolors.

Both of his parents imposed specificity. These weren't flowers in the garden but tulips, irises, geraniums, pansies, roses. His father's collection was not butterflies but spotted fritillaries, eastern bath whites, banded graylings, Adonis blues, pearly heaths, purple emperors, scarce coppers, safflower skippers. The rose he'd painted for them was not red but crimson, with overtones of vermilion. No doubt it was a precision that made it easier for him to pick up and process strange languages—the German and Yiddish of his father's customers, the French of his mother's friends, and the English he studied in books. They were not Jews, his father announced, but atheists from Jewish families. It wasn't that György felt *bored*, his mother clarified, but lonely.

At sixteen, György had enough of an understanding of war to know that the Károlyi might no longer be there, nor its tulips and irises, its rabbits and warblers. The house he'd lived in all his life, until now, might be nothing but rubble, and his family's history, their legacy, destroyed with it. His parents had relocated—he knew that much—so their bodies would not be tangled among its stones and copper and lumber. Budapest, like other great cities of Europe, might be burning now, or buckling beneath a rain of shells. Since the Reich had dispensed with allies and taken direct control of Hungary, pushing Horthy and his government aside, it was no longer possible to rely on the Hungarian papers—if they were still printing. Magda said she had faith. The Jews had made Budapest their home and it was their great capital of Europe; not even Hitler could take it away from them. They had withstood millennia of suffering that far outweighed this "German menace," and God would again pity them. Even though many Jews, in their complacency, had turned their backs on God, Magda said—and here she turned away from György, as if she didn't want to be reminded—even so, she said, He would reserve for them their place.

It wasn't until after the war that György—and the majority

of the world along with him—learned that between May 15 and July 9 of that year, 1944, the Reich had deported 437,402 Hungarian Jews, and that all but 15,000 of them were immediately sent to Auschwitz. In less than two months, more than 380,000 human beings had stepped right from the train into the gas chambers. Hungary, as one newspaper put it, had been Hitler's last act of desperation. György had to read the word again. *Desperation.* By then, he had moved out of Magda's apartment, and never found out what she thought about Budapest, about a great city for the Jews, after hearing such a story.

His parents, of course, never arrived.

═══

They were the sort of people you remembered forever:

Henry, his de facto partner in the shipyard. As a unit (or "team," as György was surprised to hear it described), he and Henry were responsible for a pallet jack someone (long fired or quit) had named Martha. Together, they spent their ten or twelve hours dragging Martha from the rail yard to the astonishing hulk of the battleship. "It didn't used to be like this," Henry often said. He was much older than György; he could have been his younger grandfather, if he weren't Black. "We watch each other now," he went on. "They call it safety, safe practices, but not so long ago you were alone. If you got hurt or crushed or keeled over, that was it." Picking through Henry's memories, György came to understand that the laws in the United States had changed. Its protections had changed. Some, of course, were taken more seriously than others, but Henry did not like to discuss the laws, the protections, that were not taken so seriously.

Magda, whose silks were thin and pale enough to inform anyone who gave them the slightest attention that they were very old,
and that she wore them as relics of a different life (a different *society*,
she would have said), where silks and hats, furs, pearls, cigarettes
from France and a case to carry them, and perfume, and fresh
flowers instead of the paper ones she'd crafted long ago and stuck
shamefully in visibly repaired vases—where all of this was money
well spent instead of money impossible, these days, to imagine.

Noël Rivers III, who inherited a town house from his father
and wasted no time in turning its ground floor into a gallery. Like
many rich people, Noël hated his father and his father's money, but
not enough to relinquish it entirely—so he spent it. "It's not as if
there will be a Noël Rivers IV," he liked to say. On György, he would
spend thousands, yet never in ways that added up to anything concrete. Unless you were to count experience, he told me. Perhaps even
confidence. Noël was anciently American ("The Riverses were the
first ones off the *Mayflower*," he lied), and yet the most European of
all Americans György would meet. Dinners, tailoring, sherry, the
new leather upholstery in the Duesenberg—nothing was ever good
enough. Nothing but certain paintings, which György, he said, had a
singular talent for identifying. "Oh, Georgie," he would one day admit, "the way you'll be remembered—it makes me positively sick, the
jealousy of it. And me, this flesh of the future forgotten. Forgive me."

The core of his life, Gil and Yvette. Both were painters, she more
talented and he more famous. Both spellbinding. "Gil," György
would learn, was a unique shortening of Guillaume, as if it were an
accident—as if one day he'd said *Bill* and someone wrote *Gil* and
all was settled. Though he'd lived in New York for twenty years,
he still seemed cripplingly French. At the time György would meet
him, Gil was in the habit of showing journalists a little picture he'd

cut from the newspaper. Whenever they asked where he was from, he'd hold up the photo of Le Havre after Operation Astonia: a vast, rolling field of mud, ruins, tree stumps, smoke. The entire town, he'd clarify—for a quote—had been destroyed by the Allies in their attempt to "retake" it. There is no *from*, he'd say, not anymore.

Yvette, to the shock of these same journalists, was not French at all but born and raised in New Haven. "My sister was Mary," she'd tell them. "My brother was Juan. I don't really know what my mother was thinking—she simply chose names she liked. Frankly, it's none of my business." Her paintings were tall and often slender, which gave them a humanlike presence on the wall. Even the abstractions seemed like individuals waiting patiently to speak with you, beings that would appreciate a moment of your time. If Gil was aggressive with paint, Yvette was persuasive; this, György would realize, was her authority. She was also a writer and spent hours with an old poet friend of hers typing and retyping and rearranging even the smallest column of print about this painter or another, this sculpture, that performance. No one took her as seriously as they did Clem or Hal but she knew—they all knew—hers was the real eye.

Clem, who would never so much as remember György's name and would invariably disparage the women he was with, even if he lauded, in print, their paintings.

Hal, one of the kindest men György would ever meet, and the first of the famous New York writers to invigorate him. In Hal's work, he told me, there was a precision and economy rare among critics; it was almost, he said, aristocratic—a hammered blade of intelligence. And deeply moral. Clem was the one who could make or break you but it was only Hal who could cast you, György would realize, into history.

The dancers—Edward, Margaret, Suzanne, Carlos, Yukio,

Claùdia, and Margot—whose entrance and exeunt, in whatever combination, into or out of the cafés and bars and clubs where Kirstein invited them, was as delicate and soundless, as beastly, as their choreographed moments onstage. With their silence and their cigarettes, they arrived and departed like clouds.

Kirstein, who looked like a statue and who often as not moved as quickly. He had a presence like a radiator, someone they all knew was there in the room—and gratefully. Even though he didn't think much of the paintings everyone else was excited about at the time, he was interested in the painters. More so, he was interested in writers, and would often suggest, to György, that he borrow this or that from the library, that he let him introduce a poet or a novelist—his treat—over a drink. He seemed to have intuited, before anyone else—even before György himself—what his life was for, and would guide it gently, like the minor adjustment of a sail on a little, lonely boat.

Monica de Trieste, who was too beautiful to be from Hoboken. She invented a name and a past and left the price tags attached to all her clothes. "Receipts," she called them. It was elegant, the tic she'd acquired whenever she threw her head back and laughed—to clutch her hand to her throat as if the joke you'd told her was so funny she couldn't breathe—but after some time György realized it was only to hide her Adam's apple.

Hofmann, in his final years of teaching. He was in his sixties and had opened his school over a decade prior, yet didn't show a single painting until 1944—the same year György arrived in New York. Not long after that, Tennessee Williams would call him "a painter of physical laws with spiritual intuition," someone who "paints as if he could look into those infinitesimal particles of violence that could split the earth like an orange." Whenever

Hofmann spoke, George told me, half the people in the room would pull a notepad from their pocket and write it down. Everyone, he said, had a Hofmann story, a quote, an aphorism, a koan. And of course a moment of shame, when they'd let the master down or embarrassed themselves in his presence. But it was only, George said, a shame all your own; Hofmann never seemed to remember, and was always ready, the next time you brought him work, to give it its fair reception.

The little group they called Three Forty-Seven, after the address they shared. Dennis's parents were rich but weak-willed and didn't know how to save him; they'd surrendered their town house and everything in it, retreating to Newport. He preferred a life, he said, filled with friends and conversation, with music. A little fun now and then, he exhaled upon György the one time they'd ridden together in a limousine. He had a weakness, especially, for poets, who fluttered in and out of his life like moonlit curtains in a dreamy breeze, he said. Not enough to have learned anything from them, apparently. Max was the only poet who seemed to last at 347, and had lived with Dennis for as long as either of them could remember. With Max came Julia, who wrote plays and complained about it, and a friend of his, Benny, who didn't seem to do anything at all. Józef, one of the most articulate and knowledgeable men György would meet in New York, lived in the attic. The latest paintings, the newest symphonies, the most recently published books—Józef knew about them and could tell you how he'd felt about them without making you feel lesser or in some way alienated if you felt differently. As discreetly as he could, György looked for clues as to what Józef did. He wanted to see his paintings or read his books or hear his music, or perhaps sit in, if he was welcome, on one of his classes. Yvette smiled and took him to a patio between two restaurants on 5th Avenue. "He's a bricklayer, Georgie."

The stranger who would fuck him in the men's toilets at the library, and whom he wouldn't see again until he was living in Paris and he appeared, one day, on the television screen, discussing his latest work of philosophy or history, it wasn't quite clear which. Nobody, before that, had used his tongue in a place György had never imagined tongues could go.

Other men, strangers and friends, rich and homeless, married and not. It wouldn't take long for György to leap out of his body and into the sublime, as he called it. There would be affairs and encounters, names and anonymity, diseases and treatments, and an everlasting tenderness that shocked him. Even now, he said, his capacity for fondness, for love, seemed unfair. Though George never clarified whether it was unfair for so much love to exist in a single man's body, or if it was unfair that so little love seemed, in comparison, spread out, shared, among the bodies of other men— that others might have been cheated in love, or deprived.

And there was Paul, whose talent and intelligence, whose genuine grace, would only touch those who knew him.

═══

After the curfews and rations of Budapest and the long, risky chain of trains, boats, wagons, and ships he'd taken out of Europe, Magda's apartment in New York felt like living in a doll's house, George told me, or perhaps a stage set where an audience was laughing at their every move. While she had her bedroom and he had his cot behind the kitchen, they did the business of living—tea, dinners, the radio she never shut off, sewing, a game of whist, even a little reading—all in one room. She called it the parlor, though György had been raised well enough to know you couldn't have a parlor without a drawing room or a library for privacy. He knew Magda would have been raised to know this as well, so he, too, said "parlor" when she asked where she'd left her glasses. The parlor had two windows that faced Clinton Street through the bars of what György initially thought was a balcony. Only when Magda scolded him—"We are simply not the type"—did she explain that this was only for emergencies. Yet that fire escape, he told me, was the best view he had of America. No one bothered him there or asked him to pay, nor did he stand out among the other youths and adults shabbily draped from building after building like damp laundry, all the way down the block. Trucks came and went and loaded and unloaded. Women struck their children and shouted things he couldn't make out. Neighbors called to each other without leaving their apartments. When a car arrived and parked in front of one of the stoops, even grown men came outside to touch it.

When Magda returned and he slipped back through the window, the parlor had never felt so claustrophobic. Then, too, it was time for tea—served hot even though it was a hundred degrees. Sometimes the oven added another ten, because one couldn't have tea, she said, without cakes. They sat sweating together, achingly civilized, and György imagined she'd been doing this for over twenty years. "I do hope they love it here," she told him while she mopped her forehead and adjusted the reception on the radio. "As much as I've come to, anyway." *They* were his parents, whom she never mentioned by name. György began to wonder if she'd forgotten them, but didn't want to test her in case it was true.

"When I first met your mother," she said one afternoon, "I'll admit I didn't know what to think. I'd never seen anyone so young and so beautiful carry herself so icily. She was a perfect frost. And your father"—she smiled—"he worshipped her. The sort of thing in a book, György. You could imagine him taking off his coat and laying it in the street, a little royal carpet for her to cross from one dry place to another." It was the first time, George told me, he'd ever seriously imagined his parents as young, which meant, too, that they'd have once been the age he was now, and perhaps just as confused and lost and lonely. But no, he realized, of course not. They'd had homes. They'd had friends. They'd had families of their own, even brothers and sisters to keep them company. The only time György had siblings, as he imagined them, was when he was very young and snuck into his mother's boudoir, where she had a great folding screen with a mirror on each panel. If he folded them all together and stood in the center, there were dozens of boys just like him. George asked them what they should do, what secrets to keep, what fort or castle to build together in their shared strength. In Magda's parlor, as she served him another cup of scalding tea, after months of silence from across the Atlantic, he felt as if he might blast apart on such a landmine of a memory. He wanted nothing more than to look into that mirror now, to fold it once more and see how that geode of brothers had grown, and to tell them not to worry, the worst was behind them, and life would only be like this a little bit longer.

———

That fall, it was clear to everyone that the war had turned, clear even to the Germans, yet there was no surrender. In György's new country, they built more cruisers and submarines, more airplanes, more guns, more bombs. They printed and filmed more propaganda and called it news, or worse—morale. Nobody knew it then, but somewhere in New Mexico the universe was being monkeyed with and what came out of it would irreparably humiliate the human desire for meaning, for purpose. But in New York, where the air began to cool and the leaves turned, György was shocked to learn that such a swamp could dress itself up so handsomely. That fall, twenty thousand people came from all over the region to watch as they flooded the dry dock and gave what would be the last American battleship to the open sea. He didn't expect such a thing to move him so deeply, and he hid his tears in his hands. But Henry, too, he saw later, had wept—and enjoyed it. "Don't ever turn away from God, Georgie. You never know when He'll touch you, and it could be some years before He comes around again."

No word, yet, from his parents, and no way of reaching them. And what would he say? I've been working. I've been making and saving money, and we'll be prepared once you arrive. The leaves here change in ways I never would have expected, there's nothing like them in Budapest. They are called maples, he'd tell them—silver, red, Norway, sugar—and London plane, honey locust, ash, hornbeam, hackberry, hemlock. Magda is what Mother would call "a frivolous person," but not unpleasantly. We walk through Central Park and I tell her which warbler has landed in front of us, or that a scarlet tanager is quite different from the common cardinal. I list these species—as I write them for you now—in English because it's impossible to translate something that doesn't exist at home, into a language that rarely leaves it. Even Magda only speaks Hungarian when she's very tired. When you arrive, I'm not sure there will be, any longer, much use for it. Not until we go back home.

He'd been walking back to Clinton Street when this letter dictated itself in his head, and he stopped in the middle of the bridge to look out over the water. From here, the skyscrapers that seemed so imposing and limitless on land were nothing—a faraway strip mine of blank rock compared to the grey hulk of the river. They just called it "East," and in fact it wasn't even a river but an estuary—another English word Americans didn't seem to know. It was as briny as the ocean and seemed as dangerous, as fathomless. A barge full of iron panels loomed below and left a trail of foam in its wake, on its way to the yard where he and Henry would cart them around tomorrow, and where one day they'd send them off to sea in the shape of a ship. Perhaps, he thought, they'd end up at the bottom of the ocean, all that work and sweat only for fish to look at. He was just tired, he told himself, then broke out into sobs that wouldn't stop. There was nowhere to hide, and he curled up into himself as he waited it out, this fit. It wasn't until he felt a hand on his shoulder that he realized someone had come close—a young man, scarcely out of his teens, György guessed, who gave him a vast smile with one crooked tooth and said, "I'm proud of you." He then helped György to his feet and walked on.

That evening, before he returned to his room, he stopped into a drug store and bought a small pad of paper and some pencils. They were nothing like the supplies he'd had in Budapest, but he was too ashamed, he told me, to ask Magda or even Henry where he could buy nicer things; he didn't want to betray any wish, any pretension. The sun was setting earlier and earlier, and there wasn't much daylight left as he sat among birds and leaves and old women in Sara Roosevelt Park and tried to recreate the face he'd just seen. I didn't dream it up, he wanted to write to his parents. They would be sitting in their room or their country hideout, wherever it was, holding György's letter together and reassuring themselves that they'd done the right thing, that they'd sent him where life was better, or at least safer. This boy said, "I'm proud of you," he'd tell them, and he helped me up, and I don't even know his name. I don't have a single friend. No one knows who I am. I almost don't exist. But he saw me.

=====

Ambitions:

To be a painter, of course. Which is different from having the ambition to paint. With the latter, there is a plasticity. An inner force (a thought, an emotion, a worldview, a suspicion, a yearning, a shame, a secret) is insistent in having an outer shape or color, a form. The ambition to paint is transdimensional. The ambition to be a painter is simply to want to be recognized for having, or wanting to have, such irrepressible will. I'm not sure—and neither is George, for that matter, since he never got the chance to know her as an adult, as a perceptive, emotionally intelligent individual— whether György's mother recognized this, or could distinguish between them, in her dotings and acknowledgments. At least once every month she'd taken him to the Szépművészeti Múzeum where she insisted he try this or that technique, just to refine his skill. He rarely listened; he'd been so sure of himself. Magda, too, would come to encourage him, though we can say without any doubt that she lacked this distinction, and that her enthusiasm for the mannerist painters at the Metropolitan Museum, and her insistence that György paint like them rather than these charlatans (with a wave of her hand: Matisse, Cézanne, Van Gogh), was borne out of her sincere belief that György could indeed become a great painter, even a famous painter, despite his obvious lack of ambition to paint.

To eliminate errors from his English. There was nothing

particularly wrong, as he learned, to have a little Europe in your vowels, even in the occasional *r* or *h*, but to use a singular in place of the plural, to drop the definite article, or to use a word like *take* when he meant *leave*—these were embarrassments he could not live with, not if he was to be taken seriously. Even Hofmann, he'd one day discover, was mocked behind his back for the rare indecipherable phrase, and by people who'd never had or even tried to learn another language—by people whose English, even, was smaller than Hofmann's, however "correct." Quickly, György learned that he could trust neither of the important people in his life. Though she'd lived in New York nearly three decades, Magda spoke like an immigrant. Nobody listened to immigrants. Neither did anyone listen to someone like Henry, whose curious use of language, no matter how much György enjoyed it, was not something he could copy. Instead, György had to eavesdrop, and spent as much time as possible, from then on, in parks and in cafés, in bars until they kicked him out for not drinking, in diners, cafeterias, subway stops, train stations. His sketches from this period are framed in idioms, turns of phrase, isolated words, as though in trying to recreate the face of his benevolent stranger, George told me, he was summoning the language he'd use to reach out to him, to befriend him.

To find this stranger. That smile. Even as the weather turned from crisp to cool to cold, György crossed the Williamsburg Bridge on foot every morning and evening. Sometimes he waited, watching the water near the shoreline factories, its ochre mix of steam and froth, glancing nervously left and right like a squirrel with a stolen meal. He studied every face that wasn't buried in a scarf or kerchief. Most belonged to the indigent and penniless—those who had no choice but to cross such a terrible place on foot instead of in the warmth of the trains howling under their benumbed or purpling toes. And what would he say? That he remembered him? That he'd been searching the city for him? That no one except his mother had ever said, "I'm proud of you," and he'd never—György didn't yet know why this was so important—heard it in a man's voice?

To have friends. Others like him, though not exactly, with whom he could walk the city's streets, comment on its strangenesses, share cigarettes, discuss ideas. He'd read a lot about friendships in books and in poems, in the published letters and journals of dead men, and wanted that for himself, the reliability of others. Someone to go out and look at the night with, to brush close to when the wind tried to separate them with its wintry chill.

To stop having a certain disturbing dream.

To at some point be married, but not right now.

To see his parents. To receive any letter at all. To know where they were.

To walk into a room and have someone there waiting, even if it was someone he didn't know terribly well, and for them to push out a chair. Some time would have passed, or maybe none at all, and this person would be happy to see him. They would want to know what he'd been up to, what he'd been thinking about—how his *work* was progressing, what he'd been *struggling* with on the canvas. In another room: another person, with other questions, other interests. To have rooms like these wherever he went, to never go anywhere lonely ever again.

THE NEW YORK SCHOOL

The Waldorf Cafeteria was on 6th Avenue and West 8th Street and buried in slums. It was, as one of the weeklies put it, the Café de Flore of New York. The emphasis, the article clarified, was on New York: grimy, steamy, full of rats, and lit like a public toilet. It was no wonder "such artists" came out of it. Whoever had written about it—George had long forgotten—carried the kind of disdain only the ignorant possess, or the reactionary. As with a scathing, uptight review of an exciting new play or novel, György wanted nothing more than to see this Waldorf—and those who drank their coffee there, who sipped their "tomato soup" of catsup and hot water.

It even smelled like a urinal. The counterman scowled at every-one, artist or not, and wouldn't tell you where the restrooms were. The patrons looked homeless. György felt overdressed and fraudu-lent, and when he came back—this time with his sketchbook and pencils—he was sure to wear his most tattered shirt, and left his boots unlaced and fanned open to simulate an age, a shabbiness, to match those around him.

He listened. It was staggering. They talked—and often laughed—about the immorality of the figure, about Kierkegaard and Hegel, the chemistry of pigments and which mediums flat-tered or offended those chemistries. War, of course. Many of them, like György, had left Europe by force, and lamented the destruction or purification or death and resurrection (depending on who was speaking) of civilization. Horsehair brushes. Humanhair brushes. The abandonment of brushes. Mustard gas, machine-gun fire, carpet bombing, shrapnel, trenches, blitzkriegs, U-boats, tanks. A new form of warfare called *kamikaze*, which György wrote in the margin of a sketch of a severe, ill-looking man he would later learn was Jackson Pollock. The end of that war. As György's first Christmas (he was shocked, in America, that it seemed so secu-lar, a holiday for everyone as long as you wanted to spend a little

money) faded into January, into February, March; as 1944 ticked
over into 1945, the end of Germany couldn't have been clearer. One
hundred thousand killed in Dresden, the papers said. What they
don't tell you, said a man György would soon know as Gil, is that
those were not soldiers but civilians. Just people. We are terrorists, this man said, and who will judge us? Auschwitz, Buchenwald, Theresienstadt, Bergen-Belsen. Zyklon B. Crematoria. The
weather began to change and the streets and parks were suddenly
vibrant—technicolor, George told me, after winter's long, grainy
silent picture, with lilacs, hawthorns, magnolias, crab apples, dog-
woods; with markets perfumed by tulips, lilies, irises, roses; and
fresh leeks, radishes, parsley, rhubarb, spinach. In Auschwitz, the
Russians found 648 bodies and some seven thousand survivors,
if the word isn't too obscene. It wasn't until later that they discovered the storehouses, with more than 1.3 million complete suits
and dresses. How was an artist, said a woman he'd soon know as
Yvette, supposed to reckon with what had happened? How does a
person go on painting? The president was dead. Berlin had been
destroyed. On the 2nd of May, they saw Hitler's severed head.
Spring had come to stay and every few days a soft, lukewarm rain
rinsed the city clean. Magazines predicted victory in the East;
the Japanese would soon surrender. The British had recorded the
liberation of Buchenwald, and when this joined the newsreels in
the movie houses some people laughed at the animated skeletons,
men and women, shying from the light. The heat had returned and
György mopped his forehead as he drew, as he listened. Had they
read Rosenberg's latest essay? Had they read Sartre's? Was Clem
out of his mind? György searched the library for these names and
read everything he could; most of it he couldn't understand but it
was exhilarating. Have you, the painters at the Waldorf asked each

other, read Burke—not the old Burke, but the new Burke? Could
you, they wondered, really give your painting a name if it meant a
suggestion, if it meant a symbol? Could you paint, thus, with language? On August 6, the United States incinerated eighty thousand people in a single blast. "Their eyes melted in ecstasy," one
man said. "It made angels out of everybody." An entire city erased
in seconds. This was something new to the earth. On August 9,
they did it again. There were shadows, they said, burned onto the
sidewalk like faces into film. Japan surrendered unconditionally.
The war was over.

His work at the shipyard came to an end and they sent him
away with a year's salary. Men returned home with money to
burn—a government program to encourage them to seek out an
education, to become men of the future. There were more people
than ever in the Waldorf. Many flung themselves at the real artists,
the practicing artists, and many you never saw twice. In Septem-
ber, someone finally spoke to him. György had been drawing and
eavesdropping among geniuses for eleven months.

"Your mistake is looking at people like shapes," she said. "You'll
never get anywhere like that. Nowhere worth going, anyhow."

She'd been watching György a long time, she went on. You get
a lot of people in here, she said, who want to be noticed, who sit
with their poetry or their drawings and get moon-eyed and im-
patient. They angle themselves so you can read or see whatever
garbage it is they're working on, and they eventually go away. "Two
things about you," she said. "You're patient. I've never seen anyone come here so long without saying a word. Which makes it extraordinary, how young you are. That's the other thing. You're . . .
what—fifteen?"

"Seventeen," György said.

"You see, that's such a shock. These other jokers—the ones I mentioned?—they're all out of college, bumming around thinking it's time to begin their lives when they've already lived their most important years. You've gotta be *young* or you get all the wrong ideas. I wouldn't say you're talented," she said, and waved her cigarette at his sketchbook, "but you definitely have discipline. You're malleable, is what I'm getting at. You should come down to the school. Hofmann—he never comes here, but you've maybe heard of him"—(he hadn't)—"he'll set you straight, or at least let you know to give up or not."

"Leave him alone, Yvette."

She smiled. "That's Gil. Come meet Gil. He's going to be famous."

$$=$$

Obstacles:

That lack of talent. Hofmann confirmed this, though so gently and so brilliantly that György felt inspired rather than crushed. György had an eye, especially for color. There was a deep appreciation of paint, its heterogeneity. Of shading and tinting and tone. But there was no will, Hofmann said. There was nothing of a flex or fight. György did not fling himself back at the world and this was why his paintings would fail. But it would be a mistake, Hofmann added, to desert his friends. There was art in his future, he said like a fortune teller, even if it wasn't the future György had imagined. "Come with me to 57th," Yvette said as they left. "We'll look at paintings and see what we think."

His youth, regardless of what Yvette had said. It *did* make it easy to notice him, but being noticed isn't precisely what sets a person apart, nor what makes them happy. A noticed person is

an object. The painters and writers he met—especially the men—
didn't listen to objects. Not objects whose voices, they said with
him there in the room, still cracked and chirped, and most notice-
ably when he spoke about something that excited him. Which of
course was when György was most vulnerable, when all of us are
most vulnerable, talking about what we love. When he followed
them to certain bars and cafés, it was anyone's coin toss whether
he'd get sent home or not, this blushing, woody insect of an "artist," whatever he'd turn out to be. He was too young, they said, for
anyone to bet on, to know where, if anywhere, he'd channel his
energy, his life force, if he even had it. "You don't talk very much,"
Gil accused, as if the men and women he now spent his days with,
morning to night and sometimes all the way to morning again,
weren't absolutely terrifying. "Where are your thoughts? Your feelings?" He was still gathering them, György. Still putting them, he
said, in order. "Timid," Gil said. "Still, you might surprise us. You
might be truly insane. I've seen it before."

An attitude or inclination toward men he was too ashamed
to label. It was, if he was honest with himself, the other reason
he rarely spoke around them. Yes, their ideas and assertions,
their philosophies, their artistic intensity, were like hot coils on
a stovetop—useful, blistering—but so too their presence in a
room, their mass and volume. Many of them were walking crises.
And they were aware, perhaps more so than György, of their gravity, their draw toward men and boys with such shame. They even
talked about these men—fairies, queers, sissies, faggots—despite
their friendships with such men. With Kirstein, for example, with
Lynes, Ossorio and Dragon, Myers, with Yukio and Carlos and Edward (it's quite possible there are no heterosexual dancers, George
told me), and later with Cage, O'Hara, Noël, Paul, and even György

when he got around to admitting it. To loving it. There would be a time, George told me, when he and Paul would hold hands in the Waldorf, and later the Cedar, just to infuriate Pollock, just to see what they could get him to do. They hadn't yet realized he was a species of murderer. But in those early days, György was behind glass and felt like an exotic, fragile bird everyone wanted to pluck bald and strangle. He felt it was wise to remain celibate forever, to live a monastic life of genius. "It's possible," speculated Claùdia, when someone brought up psychoanalysis, "to thrust all of one's deviant sexual energy through the pinhole of artistic expression. To sublimate, I think is the word, one's life into art." *Sublimate,* György wrote in his notebook—more words now than sketches. *Freud. Jung. Reich. Pathology. Castration.*

His *bourgeois* lifestyle—another word he'd written down and hidden. To live with Magda, to eat meals together, to listen to the radio and go for long, leisurely walks in beautiful places, to look through the classifieds for more "steady work," as she called it, to look at a Dughet or a Rousseau and think, *How beautiful*—this was antithetical, his new friends implied, to true feeling, to an authentic life. To be taken seriously might require a schism from his "provincial" background, the others called it, even if György was from one of the greatest cities in Europe, a much older one than New York and far richer in history. Besides, he told me, it wasn't easy to find work once the war had ended—not as an immigrant, however green your papers were. There were too many men in the city again, American men who everyone agreed were quite real, quite "all," and deserving of every chance and opportunity. His savings—the money he intended to give to his parents, when they arrived, but which more and more seemed to belong entirely, horrifically to him—would last at least a few months if he lived like Gil and Yvette, like Yukio or Margot. "Look at the greats, George," Max said. "They were hungry and desperate. They shivered all winter. They howled at the damn moon. Are these not our teachers?"

The future, but not every day. The future was always there; you couldn't get away from a thing like that. Nobody could. But it was a way of seeing it that terrified him, a glimpse he only got when he wasn't expecting it, like turning a corner on the right street and having the city line itself up perfectly, all the way to the river. It wasn't like the river went anywhere, George told me. It never got up and walked off or dried up when you weren't looking. It was just that most days you didn't worry about it. But then you'd see it, and you'd worry; and this future, too, was something that tempted you, that asked you to cast yourself into it and drown. And then you'd turn, George said, and when you looked back it'd be gone. You'd have escaped once more.

$$=$$

At that time, Gil and Yvette shared the same studio, and lived in it, too. It was a vast space not meant for them or anyone, an old warehouse not far from the Waldorf. It would've been a death trap, George told me, were there any way you could imagine such a structure destroyed. It seemed like something grown up from the rock of the island, a piece of Manhattan that'd pulled itself out of the ground. It would be there until humankind became dust, George said—or vapor, as it were. Gil had built an "apartment" within the loft, a little bedroom and living area surrounded by walls with gauzy windows to let in the light, with a kitchenette and a water closet. György wasn't sure where they bathed and didn't want to risk asking. There was no hot water, Yvette once explained as he waited, attempting to wash his hands before helping serve tea and some day-old bread. "It's a luxury we don't really need."

To live deliberately, György had taken a studio nearby. For the price and amenities—HOT WATER—he'd thought he was getting something both cheaper and more luxurious than Gil and Yvette's massive space, but he hadn't realized that "studio apartment" did not mean a studio where one painted or sculpted, or even necessarily ate meals. But it was his own space, as he'd explained to Magda, and he would always be grateful for her hospitality. "I'm sorry we didn't get a chance to sit down together," she said as he packed his things, "you and your parents and I. But I know in my heart that God has kept them safe, that one day they'll find you." Though she was smiling, even brushing at a tear in her eye, she could not help herself: "Even if they don't appreciate it, or believe it." She'd never meant to shame his parents, of course, nor György himself—but to imply offhand that, perhaps, what had happened in Germany was punishment for a people who, like György, had lost their faith. Perhaps György should pray with her, attend synagogue with her, before it happened elsewhere. Before it happened here. All the same, he forgave Magda her faith and secreted away two months' rent in a little envelope on his night table, which she'd certainly have refused under less deceptive circumstances, and called her his oldest, dearest friend.

It was just over a year since he'd arrived in New York, and he was now living alone. There was no one who'd known Budapest in his life, no one who'd known someone his parents had known. No one left to recognize the little curl in György's consonants, still evident when he drank or grew too animated about a painting or an idea. It wasn't that he felt shame, he insisted; he simply didn't want to discuss it with anyone, to share it. There was nothing more than *this*, he thought, and sat reading in his new apartment. This is how it is, he thought, and walked to Gil and Yvette's, or to the Waldorf, or met Max or Margot or Carlos for a drink, a poem, a theory. History was finished.

That winter, Yvette threw a Christmas party—more of a commentary on religious traditions, she said, than anything. Every time there was a party in New York, there was a chance someone rich would show—Kirstein or Noël Rivers or even Peggy herself. They were always interested in what the artists were doing, what their studios looked like, which paintings looked fresh and which abandoned. The artists, of course—most of them—had no money. There were no gifts. Out of craft paper, Yvette had fashioned their decorations— linked garlands of carefully taped rings, folded flowers, fans. The radio sounded as though, at one point, someone had dropped it, and no one could agree on whether or not the gin was safe to drink (which didn't matter, effectively; they drank it either way).

And then there he was, the young man with the smile. At least he assumed. He didn't seem to recognize György, which filled him with doubt. Was it really him? Nothing seemed to have changed, not his hair or the softness of his voice, not even the look in his eye. Was György so forgettable? Unlike most of the guests, rich and not, who clustered around Gil's paintings and flattered their creator, this boy stood alone in front of Yvette's work, sipping gin from a paper cup. György watched for a flash of teeth but pretended not to, nodding while Gil told an embarrassing story about Pollock who sat across from him in a folding chair, catatonic or in a ticking rage— it was hard to determine which. The chair beneath him would become a weapon before the night was over, and people would scream and others would laugh while he swung it at his friends who were also his enemies, but for the time being he just drank, one cup after another like an old, leaky motor. Yvette was standing behind Gil and running her fingers through his hair but she, too, was watching the boy from the bridge study her paintings. Obviously she knew him—it was easy enough to see—but why she should fear him, or grow nervous, was much harder to discern. He was scarcely György's age and what was there, in a boy, to be so afraid of?

"You're using your blues too decoratively," he said. He'd known she was listening and turned to give her a smile.

György shivered.

"I knew you'd say that," Yvette said.

"Because I'm right. You know you can't treat blue this way, not like the reds and yellows, not even the violets. And you feel guilty about it."

"Guilty," she echoed. She blew a cloud of smoke in his direction. "You're like somebody's mother, Paul."

Paul.

"Georgie," Yvette said. "Take care you keep that heart of yours. The worst thing is to get wise before your time and let it dry you out. Or maybe the second worst, after being right all the damn time."

Paul turned to György. "You're welcome, Yvette."

"I'll rethink the whole thing tomorrow."

"Not the whole thing; you know the rest is brilliant."

"You could *start* with that next time, you know."

Paul took her cigarette and lit one of his own and handed it back. "I do know. Thank you, my love."

Color was multidimensional, Paul began—multi*relational*—in a way that depth and line, weight, shadow, tint, and tone were not. It was like juggling ten pins instead of three, he said, which left us with a paucity (György had never heard this word) of descriptive vocabulary. Color wasn't left, or up, or thicker, or even necessarily darker; and with such a prismatic compass, he said, it was so much easier to get lost in a painting, particularly in paintings that seemed or tried to be *about* color. It was like trying to describe a smell, he said, in a work of literature. "How can you navigate," he asked György, "if you don't even know the patterns in the stars? The asterisms"—(another word)—"who narrate the way?"

A love story need not always be romantic, and in fact there were as many love stories, George told me, as there were genres of love. When Gil became belligerent and Pollock tried to fight him like a dizzy, wounded lion tamer—when the table with all the liquor and cheeses and crusty old breads went stumbling across the room—Paul took György by the hand, retrieved their coats, and led him out into the night.

The sky was right on top of them. He hadn't realized how steamy it'd been inside the loft until the winter weather washed over his prickly skin. It'd begun to snow—a wet, warm fall so slow you could pause it if you tilted your head at just the right speed, and fill the air around you with tentative, hovering flakes unsure where or whether to land. *We've made a mistake*, György imagined the snowflakes would say, *and we are very sorry, we must go back to our own heaven where we were born.* New York was always blue or grey or gold and that night it was cavernously blue. They talked about art and poetry and stupid geniuses, of the hopelessness of war and the lack of any possible future. He'd never felt so happy in his life. No, George told me, sometimes a love story was simply the tale of a true and great friendship, a friendship, he imagined, for the ages. Even if there was, he admitted, quite a yearning along with it, one that never, even now, had really gone away.

Paul recognized in György their true commonality, and as they walked—to Paul's apartment, György assumed—he grew comfortable in his decision to let go, to give in, to do whatever this boy wanted to do and live in whatever evil or pathological way there was to live, as long as it was happily. He knew, mechanically, what men did together—information pieced together from jokes at the Waldorf and secret drawings at Carlos's apartment and police reports in the newspaper, this or that man disgraced, pariahed—and knew what he wanted to try and what he found revolting to imagine, and had begun to orchestrate this in his head when Paul led him out of the snow, down the steps, and into the toilets underneath Christopher Street. For the first time, Paul gave him a very different species of smile, one that only appeared with a blush and a wink, and opened the big, heavy door. It was a long, busy stable of stall doors, some left open and some closed and nearly all of them occupied. With György's hand in his, Paul led him through the offerings until he found someone, or a particular part of someone, he could not resist. The man was older and not well cared for but that wasn't what mattered to Paul. György watched his new friend sink to his knees and swallow this stranger and felt abandoned, ashamed, and so overwhelmingly horny he was trembling with it. The other men noticed. They caught his scent. They beckoned and he neared. They unzipped and he was home. Naturally you know, George told me, how it's never enough—not after that.

═══

The gyroscopic flutter of a secret is a way of life. György felt like a wind-up toy lurching its brittle little mass across the city's streets, his clack and rattle audible to everyone. All would know he was in love.

They were always together, he and Paul. At any moment György could decide to ask him if he remembered the day on the bridge, his act of kindness. At every moment he did not. He knew he wasn't wrong. There was no way it wasn't Paul. It was about possibility, George told me, keeping alive the idea that Paul would or could remember it, such a formative moment, in the same way we do not try to succeed because we cannot bear, he said, to fail.

Paul lived in a spacious, generally empty apartment far up-town, near the university he'd stopped attending. In the central room there was nothing but a large sofa near the window, an ash-tray on the floor, a Victrola, and several crates of records. They spent whole days like that, legs tangled together on the couch, smoking and listening to music and reading until the sunlight drained from the room. The only lamp was in the bedroom, which György rarely saw. The sunset was their signal, even on the snowi-est days, to throw on their coats and take the train downtown—to the Waldorf, to Gil and Yvette's, to the bars, the coffeehouses. Peo-ple started calling them the twins, even the people who assumed they were lovers.

Which they were frustratingly not, George told me, no matter how many hints he made or situations he engineered. After they drank their martinis and critiqued some paintings and smoked their throats into sandpaper they walked side by side to another re-stroom, another alleyway, another *spot* Paul had found and wanted György to enjoy alongside him, but only alongside. The first time a man slid his cock into his ass, he'd made eye contact with Paul who, in that sodium-lit boiler room, was opening up for someone else. He didn't know what he'd done wrong. When they were alone, when they read poetry to one another, when they sat looking at paintings or snuck into theaters, Paul was meltingly affectionate.

Not even his mother had lingered on the nape of his neck or kissed the rounded tip of his ear. But when it came to the heated part, the trembling part, Paul drenched him with ice water. Stripped and debased for strangers, Paul was a different person, sometimes two at once. György began to wonder if this wasn't what all homosexuals did, even the ones you always saw together—playacting their little marriage until it was time to sin, when they would descend beneath the streets and rut like vermin. Perhaps it really was a sickness.

Paul was difficult to please, nearly impossible to impress—and of course György tried. As the winter began to weaken its grip, he still tested this or that volume of poetry, studying it himself beforehand, to try to shift their dynamic, to present the one book that Paul hadn't yet discovered. All were known or trash—most the latter. When György introduced painters they hadn't yet seen together, or Kirstein and his entourage of dancers, or any variety of poet or novelist or playwright, Paul only smiled: Yes, they'd already met, but it was lovely to be reminded. Before he left Columbia, he must have done the same, György realized, with his professors. They would never have known enough. They could never have surprised him. "A man needs to be challenged, Kertész. He needs to be throttled. And here we are coddled and spoken to like schoolchildren learning to sing the alphabet." Some people—especially the poets—crossed the street or switched tables when they saw Paul approach. There were nights when he could clear a room by ordering a drink, everyone too wounded to deal with him. It made György crave that kind of power, which he translated as respect. Like Yvette, Paul had authority, and you either faced up to it or ran away. György wanted to know what that felt like—to will others into awe.

"I think part of what I'm for," Paul said to him one late winter day, "is for us to determine what's to be done with your life. I think that's why we met." They'd gone for a long walk to enjoy the sun and were somewhere, George told me, along the Hudson. He remembered the shimmer of the water, like dropped silk, and his feeling of transience, even intrusion. It'd never occurred to him to think of life as something to be done with.

Was György interested in music? He never knew how to respond to or engage with that word, *interested*—yet he supposed that he was. As the months unfolded into spring, Paul took him to the bars north of his apartment where there was jazz every night. At first, György felt too conspicuous to enjoy it the way Paul seemed to, as if they didn't deserve to hear it and someone might say this, might ask them to leave. Yet no one spoke to them at all, nor asked their ages as they ordered liquor in various regrettable combinations. He began to appreciate it, even find great pleasure in it—how sometimes a song he'd heard before stretched itself out or wandered in circles, looking for itself, reflecting on who it used to be. Like the paintings downtown, these songs quoted themselves, they quoted their friends. They shared a vocabulary but György wasn't sure, yet, what it was. One trumpet player, a man named James, began to notice them and nod in their direction. He spoke to them sometimes at the end of the night, too drunk to be on guard, and spoke of the *feeling* of jazz, of it moving around in his body and slithering through the floorboards and crawling up the walls. What did György have to say about this? What did he have to contribute? Many of the men and women who dragged themselves onstage and channeled this music through their bodies were laced with bruised veins and offered such sad, unsalvageable eyes. His notes from this period are a tangle of sketched limbs and sweat with garlands of extraordinary rhymes, words he'd never thought could meet. Theirs was a shocked and mutilated avant-garde, George told me, and he was afraid it would prove too magnetic to resist.

There were events, Paul said later, almost theater but not theater exactly, that György might find interesting. If you were in the right place at the right time, you could see people hurt themselves, or sob without provocation, or simulate childbirth with fruits and vegetables. Most of these curiosities were downtown, often on subway platforms or in between warehouses and tenements. It might be raining or upsettingly cold but often these actors, or performers, perhaps artists, would still strip down to their underwear and slather themselves in mud, trash, and gutter water, howling like dogs. Without tracking their patterns, George told me, it would have been easy to assume some virus had entered the city water and was turning people mad. But this was only shock, and shock never lasts. In the beginning, there were people who drenched themselves in paint and walked up and down Houston or Canal Street, and people stopped and looked—one man even took pictures—but within a few weeks no one looked, and the only people who photographed it were the people who arrived with the walkers, the assistants or friends or simply the people who'd walk next time. Somebody tried to call it abstract humanism but nobody wanted to repeat it, and one day there were no walkers, and nobody mentioned it again. Many of these events, George told me, were like this—little moments that came and went and seemed to get forgotten with the same velocity of their sudden, unwanted births. They fell into niche, closed audiences of documentarians— people to record and no one else. He appreciated them, he told Paul, and he thought about them, but there wasn't anything to say, he said, or to add. Anyway, he couldn't risk arrest—he might get sent back to a country that was no longer his, and all would be lost.

Then rain, then heat. Summer had come to punish them. Paul was still restless. It'd begun to seem as if he were looking for a way to get rid of him—to pawn me off, George told me, as we used to say. "What about photography?" Paul asked as they drifted through the halls and ornate stairways of the Whitney. He knew someone with a studio and dark room not far from here, in fact quite close to György's apartment, if György were interested. They walked over. She even had a spare Leica II, as it turned out, and seemed unperturbed by Paul's insistence that they borrow it, despite György's embarrassment. She was used to him, György noticed, and—as with all of Paul's acquaintances—he wondered where and when they'd met, under what circumstances. It was hypocritical, of course, since he'd scarcely told Paul a thing about his own life (Paul never asked), but it maddened him to not know where the most important person he'd ever met had come from, how he'd been raised, what was expected of him. The first photo he ever took was of Paul, a blurry, off-center shot of him laughing as this photographer—George had forgotten her name—told him an old joke they shared, a joke György could not have understood. An intimacy to which György did not belong.

It gave them an excuse to walk. To look. A crooked scattering of cigarette butts like gassed insects beneath a park bench. Irises— attenuated, inked with shadows, their heads hung in shame or sadness. A blur of a boy, too swift to be caught in focus, who'd found a length of pipe and was beating a fire hydrant in desperation. A spackling of discarded sandwiches, shredded and shat on by pigeons. Imbricated sheaves of mottled, moldy playbills—*Antigone* at the Cort Theatre. A river that looked nothing like dropped silk. Crowded power lines—toothy, beaded necklaces of birds strung over the street.

Later:

Paul draped naked on the floor, face buried in his forearms as he listened to a record. Paul hiding his face with a volume of Rimbaud. Paul stepping out of his shower. Paul asleep, Paul awake, Paul aflame as he lit a cigarette in the dark. The sliver of shadow Paul's tooth made when he smiled in the right light. Together, they watched them emerge beneath the hydroquinone like drowned memories washing up on a gunmetal beach. "This is my favorite shadow in the world," György said, pointing to the cleft where the backs of Paul's thighs met, and laughed when Paul smacked him on the back of the head. They found these photos easy to take, and a little collection of them began to grow in a secret folder hidden among Paul's records, images they would spread on the floor and critique as if paintings before visiting the toilets in Central Park. It was a foreplay, George told me, but there was a deeper pride; he was making, he said, things he admired, populating the world with little objects of beauty, even if they were just copies of Paul's beauty. And even if, he added, they weren't exactly photos he could share. None of it was journalism and there was no use for it in the world, but they existed all the same.

Sort of like, he added, how he and Paul were not together, but together all the same. Which had only deepened with the presence of the Leica, which seemed to simulate a third person in the room and which performed the same function, George said, as that third person—to allow Paul to be naked, to be needy, in front of György in a way that György could not touch. It brought them closer, which gave Paul an excuse to be further out of reach. Yet it also gave György an excuse of his own, to be present and not present— to show up at Gil and Yvette's, for example, and watch one or the other paint, listen to them argue, and to photograph the way their fingers clung to a brush or how they flicked turpentine across a

canvas. Even if he never became a photographer, George told me—
not in the way anyone, at that time, might have expected—being
"the man with the camera" taught him how to watch, which is a
way of being kind to the lives of others.

In July, Paul said it was time to get away. "You can come with
me if you like. I just need a break from the city, from the heat." It
was such a Paul thing to say; it made György want to refuse, to
dignify himself with plans or ideas, he couldn't possibly join him.
But he said yes. He didn't realize there was no "away" to go to,
not exactly. Since Paul's parents evidently paid for Paul's apartment (never discussed, but Paul did not work and seemed to have
very little spending money), György assumed there would be a
cottage or country home. Instead, when Paul arrived at György's
apartment, it was in a borrowed car full of canned food, books,
and camping equipment. He hadn't even realized that Paul had a
driver's license, or that he could bear sleeping outside. "I was an
Eagle Scout, Kertész," Paul said. It was a term György had never
heard before and he wasn't sure, exactly, what it meant.

It took the better part of the day to get to the Catskills, especially
at Paul's pace. Initially, he'd feared Paul would be reckless with such
a machine, but he was slow and careful—a leisurely drive. Instead of
a flaneur, he said, "I suppose I'm something of a *driveur*." As in the
city, he enjoyed detours and interruptions; he liked to look carefully
at things he'd never seen or given attention, and encouraged György
to take pictures. Advertisements for farm eggs with illustrated hens
offering, in feathered hands, their own ova. Roadside restaurants
that promised fresher coffee than other roadside restaurants (left
unnamed but libelously suggested). Ash and birch trees leaning
away from the road, as if repulsed by its reflective heat. They looked,
György thought, as if they wanted to pull up their roots and scurry

down toward the Hudson, which here seemed an entirely different river. Mansions, shacks, cottages, farms, cabins, estates—whoever had got here first, that was who built it. As they turned away from the river the soil began to thin with vast pale stones like the bald patches on a burned scalp, like a war injury. Pines—György didn't know their names and felt ashamed of this imprecision—began to climb up out of the deciduous clusters. You never told me it would look like this, he imagined writing to his parents, even if he knew, by now, they would never read it. They'd never cared for, perhaps never even acknowledged "the country," and in György's imagination—he hadn't realized it until now—the country was little more than space between buildings, parkland that simply went on for miles instead of blocks. But this was no Károlyi.

They'd seen nothing, he realized then. Not a tree. Not a field. Not the ruined wall of an old village. There were no windows on a cattle car. He felt sick, he told Paul—"Please stop the vehicle"— and he climbed down into a ditch where he sobbed alone. "So many sharp turns," he said when he returned.

They established themselves in a little meadow by a creek, cradled in evergreens that stretched over a hundred feet into the sky— hemlocks, Paul confirmed. The day had cooled, a break in the summer heat that György didn't realize, at first, was a shift in elevation. Paul became someone else. He set up their tent and established boundaries, spaces, zones, rules—they were to sleep here, keep their personal items here, wash in the creek, cook and relieve themselves as far from the tent as possible, even in the middle of the night, and never let the sun set without gathering as much wood as they could carry. György did not sleep, not with a night full of owls and rodents and coyotes, and not with Paul's dreams swimming just beneath his eyelids. In the morning he was slow and stupid, intolerant with Paul's orders, and went off by himself to wish he'd lived differently, that he'd gone to some other country and tried harder to be a painter. In Paris, he thought, he'd have sold a painting by now, he'd have met the right people, he'd be discussed in cafés and celebrated when he walked into a room, not this invisible immigrant no one wanted hanging around. If he killed himself, he thought, right now—if he found a cliff and leapt off of it—nobody would miss him, not even Paul.

He woke around noon, alone on a tuft of grass and with ants in his hair. It was a beautiful world and he was happy to be in it. He hadn't realized it, how tired he'd been and how foolish the mind can become, and made his way back to their camp. Paul was stretched out reading by the creek. Not even a greeting. György was starving but too ashamed to ask and flipped through the books he'd brought along with him. All of it was too tiring to read, too much English for his brain to handle. Instead he took up his camera and photographed the forest around him. It lost its depth in the viewfinder, a flattened plane of gradients, shapes, and shadows flung out in front of him, an abstract in its own way that would lose even its color when developed. So too the monarchs with their wings like Tiffany lamps, or the baby-blue finches and their flashy flecks of orange as they shot from one branch to another. For the first time in his life, a nest of robin's eggs, the most peaceful blue in the world. He put the camera away and vowed to remember it, these colors, the way some fool, George told me, vows to remember a smell.

That night it was exceptionally cold, and Paul joined him in his sleeping sack. "This isn't a trick," he said as he helped György undress, then shucked off his own clothes, down to his bare skin. "It's the best way to keep warm." In seconds he was straining and felt Paul flex against him, the contraction that began, in every man, somewhere at the root of his pride and rippled outward along his perineum. "As friends?" Paul asked, and they panted like dogs as they helped bring each other off. György slept without interruption, without even a dream.

It was the tenderest time of their lives together. If, as I've said, *together* is the word. They read to each other and played cards and went for long walks in the forest. György took fewer and fewer pictures, and those he did take were of Paul. They lounged naked like sprites and shivered in the creek. Paul taught him how to fish and György cried when he pierced the poor creature behind the eye, as Paul instructed, and held it to the board alive as he began to fillet it. It gaped in horror but Paul told him not to worry, it felt no pain. They did not fish again, and washed wild raspberries in the creek and ate cans of beans and vegetables and corned beef, and laughed at how raucously they'd begun to fart day and night. One night, around the fire, Paul read a poem aloud, something György hadn't even known he was working on, a beautiful poem, George told me, the most beautiful poem he'd ever heard, or at least that's what he'd believed at the time. Love is like that, George told me, and theirs was, as I've said, a love story. He'd give anything, he told me, to remember that poem, to be able to read it again, but he'd laughed all the same, along with Paul, at their mutual recklessness, their rebellion, their indifference, as Paul handed the poem to the fire and watched it grow its phoenix wings and flit off into the night.

＝

Their first ending, as friends, happened after their return to the city. Paul had taken him to see a film—*The Flying Serpent*. It was something Paul had meant to laugh at, to mock, but it was a film that changed György's life. It was where, as George himself liked to say, George Curtis was born. I didn't learn until much later that this was only half true, that his story was in fact much sadder, but I didn't trouble him with this contradiction; we all have the right to believe in ourselves.

It wouldn't have happened, George admitted, without the newsreel beforehand. The war had been over for a year, the newsman said, and the United States was stronger than ever. Nothing in history had rivaled the power of the American military. This was evident in Hiroshima, and on-screen György saw burned and scarred human beings, men, women, and children mutilated by the bomb. What was once a city, surveilled from the sky, was now a flat plain of rubble. People were blind and half-melted yet composed in their agony, and with their irradiated bodies waited in line for American soup, American bread, American bandages, American morphine. They watched American movies and looked at the pictures, George said, in American magazines.

The screen then jumped to another locale—a ring of tropical islands wavy with palms, and an ocean full of warships that bobbed like bath toys. "Here is the motion picture spectacle of our time," the newsman said, and explained that the countdown the audience heard was announcing the latest test, conducted just last month in the South Pacific. It was, George told me, the first time he would see one of the most famous explosions on earth, an explosion so iconic it would one day become visually synonymous with the phrase *nuclear weapon*. From the middle of the open ocean, a blast spread up and outward, with a ring of water and vapor belting around its bulk. The blast, the newsman chirped, destroyed even more ships than they'd hoped, and sent fifteen-foot-tall radioactive breakers to the beach almost four miles away.

No trace of the *LSM-60*—the decommissioned landing ship from which they'd lowered the bomb into the water—was ever found.

The island itself, he did not say, was no longer habitable, and its inhabitants had not yet been told this.

The film they watched afterward took on a new meaning. György sensed this even without having seen it before. *The motion picture spectacle of our time.* He felt shaken, altered—all the things Paul said art was supposed to do, and he knew that films like these, with their space aliens and plagues and ray guns and radiation, could shake and alter others if they were good enough, powerful enough. If they were, in a word, art. But the gap, George told me, between that level of art and who he was at the time, a boy from Hungary who wouldn't even turn eighteen for another two months, seemed helplessly unbridgeable. What he needed to say, he needed to say *now*, and when the movie was over he excused himself and wrote line after line of a poem, his first attempt in months, and went to the Waldorf where he drank coffee all night as he revised and transcribed it onto a fresh page.

In the early morning, without sleep, he walked uptown and showed it to Paul.

"Is this a parody?"

"The picture we saw yesterday," György said. "All of it—it made me think."

Paul flipped the page over as though an explanation were on the back. "This is not thinking."

"But what do you think?"

"I think you're terrible. Please don't ever put a pen to paper again—you'll be doing us all a favor, especially yourself."

"That's very cruel, Paul."

"There's nothing cruel in honesty. You showed me the poem. Do you want me to lie? To say it's profound? To say you have talent?"

"Paul."

"It may not seem like it, but I take my work very seriously. That's different, in case you can't quite comprehend this, from taking *myself* very seriously. I don't take myself seriously at all. I think that's where you go wrong, friend. You have this vision of yourself—"

"Never mind, Paul."

"No, you have this vision of yourself—"

"No." György took the poem from Paul's hand and folded it into his pocket. His hands were trembling and he knew the moment he stepped into the hallway he'd start to cry, but he was surprised, then, at his own strength. "I'm sorry I bothered you. I won't be doing it again."

"You wanted me to be honest," Paul said. "I told you what I think. Don't be such a child. Go home, get some sleep, and we'll go out later. We'll see Gil and Yvette."

"Yes," György said, but he did not see Paul again that evening—and in fact not for several months, and only then, deep into winter, at the Waldorf one evening. Paul was sitting alone with a blank notebook, listening to the conversations around him. They were cordial and talked about the death of Bonnard, shared a cigarette (Paul was out), and separated as they left. They were diminished, a print set too close to a sunny window. Long ago, he'd burned the poem—Paul was right—but he couldn't erase it from existence. He couldn't let go of what he'd wanted, nor how badly he'd wanted Paul to want it for him. It would sit between them as long as they both lived.

======

It was a period of change:

Without Paul, he spent more time with Yvette. Gil's paintings were beginning to sell and he'd taken his own studio, which also meant, Yvette said, that he was taking even more lovers than usual. "It doesn't bother me as long as I don't meet them," she told György—and, by default, Hal, who was there listening. She'd decided to do a series of portraits of people she thought exceptional, and Hal was the first. "No one's helped me see more *seeingly*," she said—a tone which may have had the tint and shade of a joke.

It was the first time György had met the writer, even though he'd been reading his work in all the magazines for over a year. Hal was cautious but observant and he saw, in the tenderness of György's vocabulary, its respect and its patience, something to cultivate. He provided assignments. "You're missing a few dimensions," he said, and gave György a library list—books to constellate his imagination, his eye. They were footholds, George told me, and for the first time it felt as if he were decoding or deciphering the way certain paintings or pieces of music struck him, the way they seemed always to have been there but as seed and not blossom.

When György, out for a drink with Hal—or in Hal's case, a half dozen drinks—mentioned the photographer from whom he'd borrowed his Leica, Hal was intrigued. *Photography?* He looked at him as if for the first time.

It was my gift, George told me, or my thanks. Hal had never considered photography before—this medium of journalists and fashionistas. Years later, when George was living in Los Angeles, he read Hal's great essay on photography and the figure of the photographer. It was Hal's translation, for a trusting audience, of a mechanical medium into an artistic one. George felt proud. It's a reward of growing old, he told me, to be able to reciprocate, to give back to our great givers.

Meanwhile, György lived. He met people and learned about what they did, most of them artists or performers but so too prostitutes and psychologists, unlicensed chemists, men who worked in banks, janitors, waitresses, and barmen, one man who called himself a wizard, an FBI agent (perhaps), and of course the New York rich, nouveau and ancien, who did nothing at all. Gorky killed himself. Wyeth painted *Christina's World*. Kahlo, it was said, had been confined to her bed and would paint her final paintings in unbearable pain and sadness. The United States had involved itself in something called "police action" in Korea—which was *not*, the president stressed, by any means a war. György spent his afternoons in the movie houses and took long walks afterward. It meant something, in a film, for the sky to burn or the stars to fall, for monsters to rise up out of the deep and tear cities to pieces with their radioactive claws. More precisely, George told me, it meant something for people to love it, to be thrilled by it. It had political dimensions, as well as spiritual. There had to be a way to take this seriously and to convince others to do the same, but every time he brought it up with Yvette or with Max and Julia they dismissed him. "Go to Hollywood if that's how you want to waste your life," Julia said, and immediately complained that her latest play had closed in only a week because of "that California brainlessness."

Zelda Fitzgerald died, and Solomon Guggenheim. Klaus Mann. Celan's "Todesfugue" appeared—in German, frightfully. György's savings dwindled and he took odd jobs—an afternoon hanging paintings at a gallery, a month typing bills of lading for a pallet manufacturer, a week providing a visitor from Boston with some young company. One of Yvette's *Hal* series was on view at the Modern; they would almost certainly purchase it, she told everyone. They did not. Later, Dalí's *Christ*. The death of Wittgenstein. Of Gide.

At lunch with Hal and Monica de Trieste, he met Noël Rivers III. György recognized instantly Noël's proclivities. "This one tells me"—Noël gestured at Hal—"that you know a painting when you see it. I'm looking for something specific but I have no idea what it is. Perhaps you could help me?"

"Georgie can help anyone," Monica said. "But he's different now. He's going to write for the movies."

Hal set his drink on the table. "You never mentioned this to me. Say more."

"There is very little to say," György replied. "I'm . . . there is— I'm not sure it could be explained. Every time I try, someone tells me I'm wrong."

"Perhaps you are. But I mustn't discourage you—an old habit. You were right about photography, after all. But . . . the *movies*?"

"I know there's something important here," György said. "And I know there's a way I can convince you of that. I just haven't found it yet. I'm . . . it's what you always say about the door. I haven't found the door, the way in. Just the windows. I'm still peering inside."

"Perhaps there is no door at all with that nonsense," Noël said.

Monica put her hand on the table. "Mr. Rivers, if Georgie says there's a door—"

"Did you know that in Italy," Noël said, "where the rather damp city of Trieste is in fact located, they say *di* and not *de*, Miss Trieste?" He turned to face György. "Perhaps there *is* a door to the movies. Perhaps there's a great palace behind that door. But right now, while you're leaving handprints and steam all over the windows, perhaps paintings are your life. Which is what Hal has told me, and which is why I asked him to put us in touch. I really am interested, Mr. Kertész."

György assumed that it wasn't about paintings at all, and when he visited Noël's town house on East 72nd he willed himself into the mood. He did, of course, need the money—especially now. Drinking his champagne, he put himself in touch with his body and told it that pleasure was a choice, and that *we might as well enjoy our work.* But Noël wanted nothing of the kind, and showed him the gallery he'd begun to assemble—still empty. "It's a secret," he said, "but we're going to have a show. I don't want anyone to know anyone, no recognizable names. We're going to shock the city. Can you do that?"

He knew some artists, György told him, and they began their work together. His salary shook him. For the first time since he'd come to New York, György could afford clothes, books, music. He wasn't terribly passionate about his work, but he could dine in restaurants and drink what the waitstaff recommended. He could afford a much larger apartment—an enormous cube of a thing he modeled after Gil and Yvette's loft—where he entertained the idea that he might take formal or composed photographs. He was shocked to fall in love with things like chairs and stereo systems and little crystal decanters, and watched Noël for his approval when he invited him over—and corrected accordingly. Noël read the spines of the books he'd collected, many of them on Hal's recommendation. "Are you *trying* to get on McCarthy's list, my friend?" he asked, and gave György a wink.

If György led Noël through the city's viscera of painters and sculptors and poets, collecting as they went, Noël showed György the airiness of New York's lungs—its ballet, its orchestra, the operas and plays, clubs and saunas. He began to recognize a plié to applaud and an allongé to pretend had never happened, an actress to adore and one to dismiss with a wave of the hand. One evening, he saw a performance so brilliant that it would take a decade, he told Noël, for another Blanche DuBois to even dare step onstage. "Ah, yes," Noël said. "One never forgets the first time one sees Madeline Morrison. Like weeping at the light from a stained glass window." They saw her again the following night and György carried in his memory a vision of her like a celestial phosphorescence in their vile earthly midst. He learned that she did movies as well, and scanned the weeklies for the programs at the movie houses. At one cinema in particular, she seemed to be a favorite. The proprietor was another man whose soul György could see without trying, and who, unlike Noël, did not hesitate to express his affection. In the slow hours, they watched the films together, even though this man, Howard, had seen them all dozens and dozens of times. He could quote them like poems. Even his hands quoted them, gesturing and fluttering as Madeline's hands had done, and with an eerily identical grace. "I don't know where she came from," Howard said, "but I hope she never returns."

He never told Noël or Howard—or anyone, for that matter—about the alleyways and toilets, the unlit spots in the parks, the paths under bridges or along seaports. In fact there was a unique and growing pleasure, George told me—which, of course, he implied, I could not recognize, not being the young age I was and of my generation and seeing, so young, what I had seen—there was a growing pleasure, he repeated, in this anonymity. Several times, György caught himself smiling at a party or ballet or art opening, sitting there with his champagne or his martini. Nobody could know, he thought to himself, about what he'd just done, about what he carried swimming inside him. It was an almost excruciating excitement to be among the rich, among the civilized, a used and fucked thing put away wet, his legs trembling, his lips swollen.

It was his own private science fiction film. He was the transdimensional being whose two realities could never quite intersect, smuggling its moist, soapy life from one universe into another.

It was from this other dimension, deep underground, that Paul returned to his life. It was 1951 and they hadn't seen each other in four years. Or perhaps they had and György had not realized it, for Paul was no longer ostensibly Paul, not in the way he remembered. He'd lost the roundness in his cheeks and the pride somewhere between his shoulder blades. For those strange men in those acrid places, he bent over less joyfully—a look of dutiful concentration in place of the smile György had so loved to watch unfurl—yet he bent, or knelt, all the same. While György enjoyed his transient partner in a corner, Paul was the sad, industrious center of attention. He couldn't ignore it, and invited him out for a coffee.

Their rekindled friendship was uncanny, as if replaced with an analytical imposter. They talked about art and listened to music and cruised all over the city; they spent time head to toe on the couch and read excerpts from favorite or terrible books. According to the painters and dancers and musicians in their circle they were "back together." But it was György's apartment, now, where they spent their private hours. It was György's money that bought their nights out.

All of that, however, George said, was nothing, absolutely nothing, compared to Paul's eyes. He'd fallen deep into the well of himself, and even though there was no voice calling out from within, even though he didn't ask for it, here was evidently some soul to save. It wouldn't be his first friend lost to heroin, but as carefully as he looked he saw no signs, no marks, none of the sleep sweats, and certainly none of the incapacitations men on opiates tend to experience; Paul, in his assignations with strangers, was as quick and as refractory as he'd been when they'd met. So it wasn't heroin. Once, in the heat of a morning, he suggested they take pictures like they used to, and helped Paul undress. Yes, he'd changed, but so too had György, if he was honest with himself, heavier and sturdier, a diamond of chest hair. Paul had grown a little dark triad of fuzz at the base of his spine, just above his ass, which György could not help but kiss. Paul dismissed it with a laugh—an actual "haha," George told me—and rolled onto his back. His cock was beginning to harden and neither seemed dissuaded or hesitant, and they had, George told me, a nice time of it. It was only later, as these scenarios repeated and accumulated, as they went further, that it began to feel wrong. Soon he felt that Paul finally belonged to him, and he was relentless in his efforts to hear Paul enjoy it, to hear Paul cry out in pleasure. Instead, Paul became more and more György's doll or receptacle, and before long wasn't even hard while György fucked him, and said nothing, and held absolutely still while György said he loved him and was so happy they were finally together and how sexy it was to finally be inside of him, to have this beautiful body, and to fill him up over and over, that was all he needed, wasn't it? while Paul said nothing as György kissed the knobby vertebra at the base of his neck.

Of course I had no idea, George told me—and wouldn't meet my eye for the rest of the day.

Noël didn't care for him. "He's like a vampire," he told György. "There's something evil about him, perhaps something dead." What else could he do? György laughed and said Paul was simply someone who grew on you, but from then on kept them apart. With Noël he went to opening night and with Paul he went to a third or fourth performance, relishing the added thrill of knowing he'd seen it before, this ballet or opera or play, while Paul was sitting there experiencing it, being exposed to such wonder or beauty— even shock—for the first time. And yet nothing seemed to move him. Nothing seemed to matter. Even György's talk of science fiction, which he only brought up to incite an ire, an old disdain he was surprised to miss, met only indifference. "You seem so sad, Paul," he said as they walked back to his apartment. Back *home*, György thought, and had come to imagine them living there for a long time, "roommates" who were always together, who simply appreciated the intelligence and charm of one another's company.

"I am sad," Paul said.

"Why? Things are so wonderful. Everything's so beautiful."

"I know."

"Then why be so melancholic?"

He didn't answer. Instead he pointed to one of their stairwells, and they walked down together. György tried to initiate with Paul while other men watched but Paul moved away. He reached for another man—something György had not watched in several months—and showed this other man joy. Paul smiled and whispered in this man's ear. The man looked at György, who was now at the mercy of some other man whose face he didn't bother to register, a man even younger than he whose cocksucking wasn't anything to swoon or moan about but who might finish the task all the same. György was trembling as Paul turned around and backed into this man's crotch. The mechanics of beginning, like oiling a motor or fixing a watch, and soon Paul was rocking against him, his eyes on György's, his cock hard and flinging its drool in thin luminescent ribbons. It wasn't a common trick, at least not with Paul, but he managed all the same: that drool went milky as he moaned and panted, as he emptied himself all over the men's room floor simply because some stranger had hit the right spot, something György, in all his sweaty efforts, had never managed. He pulled out of his eager stranger's mouth and went home, locked the door, took a pill, and went to bed.

⸻

It wasn't intentional, George told me. He hadn't meant to never see Paul again; it was simply what happened, the way it worked out. In his imagination they would keep their distance for a few days, maybe a week, and György would call and invite him for coffee or a drink or a long walk and they'd talk over their relationship, if the word wasn't too loathsome. Perhaps we weren't meant to be lovers, György would admit, and suggest that they remain friends, that they go back to how things had always been. But when he called, the number had been disconnected. His apartment was suddenly vacant. It hadn't even been a week, George told me, and Paul had erased himself from New York. He was furious. He was crushed. It felt, he said, as if he'd lost everything.

Most of all, he was relieved.

It was a month before he received Paul's letter. I imagine you're very angry w/ me, it said, & I wouldn't—or don't, or can't—blame you for that. I would be angry w/ me, too, & in fact often am— quite angry—w/ myself. I don't like myself—is that so strange? I never have. Often this isn't a problem—I live w/ it like a disease or a limp. Yet sometimes it worsens—to tell the truth it becomes unbearable—I find myself looking at tall buildings or bridges—at deep water—at blades & poisons. You know what I mean, Georgie. But that's really not what I want for myself, I promise. I promise that's not how I want to go. If I ever do it, you know that—it's not at all what I wanted & I'm sorry—I'll have let you down but it won't be what I've wanted. I hope I don't let you down!

Part of that hope, the letter went on, has been escaping—some time out, as it were. I've gone to live w/ my parents—which has its price, of course. Hence the P.O. box. Please please please only write to this P.O. box. Do not seek out my parents or their address or things will only get worse. I'm just here to relax, to get myself together, to calm down—I haven't felt like myself in a long, long time, Georgie—if I even had a self—who's to say? Anyway, like I said, keep this an absolute secret.

I'm so sorry about what happened. I didn't mean it. I wasn't myself—just overwhelmingly sad, which isn't so much like being morose but like being unable to breathe—& I want to breathe again. I'll see you in a few months, my friend. In the meantime, take care, keep working, & tell me everything. Yours.

George showed me the letter. It was well kept yet well loved. There was a reverence about it, and a terrible threat of being lost. "It doesn't take much," George told me as he folded it back into its place, "to vanish from this world, and from history altogether."

=

New York without Paul:

Colorless. He told Paul this, in one of his many letters. And it isn't, he wrote, simply because of all the Klines, I promise. You remember them, all those arcs and smears of black. They're famous now. I convinced Noël to purchase one of the big ones and ever since they're all people want. No, what I mean is that nothing is vibrant any longer. Which is perhaps how it was for you, I admit, for a very long time. Is it any consolation that, as dull, as black and white, as life may have been, you did bring me color? And so much.

A labyrinth, with no way out. György had developed the habit of sifting through his old photographs, and occasionally developing newer, larger prints of the ones he liked. The ones he could sell—ones that were not Paul, if it needs to be said—he tried selling but no one was interested, not even Noël. "Just because you have an eye doesn't mean you can turn it on yourself." Sometimes, he confessed in a letter to Paul, he didn't think he'd ever have the talent he'd always craved, the talent he felt like he needed just to survive. His favorite photographs, and by extension his favorite memory, was that week he and Paul had spent in the Catskills, an openness and a silence that made New York seem suddenly intolerable. Paul on the tuft of grass they'd pressed flat, giving the Leica a strange little grin. The idea that such a person was ill, that he might die of sadness, left György restless and helpless and trapped. I'm scratching at the walls, he wrote to Paul. When you were here, I barely knew there were walls at all.

Repetitive. Oscillating between two lives, neither felt real, and each day felt like he'd been swatted from one to the other and back and would never *arrive*, meaning he would never live. In the cinemas and on his walks afterward, or sitting in the sauna at Noël's health club where György could only join him as a guest, he imagined what this Hollywood was like, if it was really so vile, so banal, as they all said. He thought of all the seismic shifts in art history, all the styles or mediums that weren't art until much later, that were "entertainment," or merely technology. I can *see* it, he thought, but I cannot describe it, and he carried this black hole around inside him until he felt alone in the universe, everything else too far to reach, out of range of even the most powerful radio signal.

Aggravating, a performance. It may have been the newfound attention and press, but most of his friends seemed as if they were reciting lines, not speaking. They imagined themselves being recorded or observed, being remembered. Even the younger painters, who'd begun to collect around Gil like streaky solvents to his drain, carried themselves like watched celebrities and future geniuses. They drank and fought and poisoned one another's reputations, not to mention their confidence. "He loves it," Yvette told György. "Of course he paces up and down and swears that he just wants to paint, he wants to be left alone and this and that, but he loves the attention, the worship." But it doesn't affect him, György wrote to Paul. Not his work. As a person, perhaps it does, but what does that matter? His paintings are as careful and meticulous as ever; he paints and destroys and paints and destroys until someone takes it away from him, and it's always something we've never seen, he wrote. In truth, György spent much more time with Yvette than with Gil, as he'd always done. If it weren't for Yvette, he'd have never met any of them, never been a part of any of it. They were beginning to pay her more, the magazines and periodicals, and occasionally she was able to rake in a little money from teaching a class or a workshop. She wasn't Gil, George told me, and in fact if it weren't for Gil everyone would have seen that. They would have seen Yvette then and not afterward, long afterward. I suppose, George told me, she is my oldest friend. It shocked him that he'd never thought of it that way before, but then a good friendship is perhaps one that never prompts such reflections, or rarely. It exists with you, not apart. Not perceived.

Lonely, above all, which he could not extinguish or assuage. He read alone and went to movies alone and watched Yvette paint without someone there to feel him thinking, someone whose thoughts he could feel unfolding in silence. With Noël his conversations were erudite and intelligent but soulless. There was no intimacy, something he hadn't realized would hurt so much to live without. No touch on the arm, no shoulder or chest to lean against. No heartbeat or breathing to hear and no body heat to smell. Of course he could have, George told me, but it would have seemed as transactional as their working relationship. And it would have shattered Noël, someone who prided himself on his restraint, his aristocratic dignity. In the definitions of his world, George told me, Noël was a saint for choosing not to abuse his privilege as a younger, prettier man's source of money. You could feel it vibrating out of his core, George told me, how badly he wanted you to know that he wasn't asking, he wasn't suggesting, he wasn't staring, he wasn't going to make you uncomfortable. When he was drunk (often), this tension increased to a ring or a drone you could almost hear, until Noël was sweating with piety, with chastity. The closest he ever came to infringing upon György's imagined sanctity was when they discussed the future, whatever that was supposed to be. "Are you thinking of taking a wife in the next few years?" he asked, and György pointed out that Noël Rivers III did not have a wife. "No, I don't," Noël admitted, "but I have money."

Lonely, György wrote to Paul. It's so much worse than I imagined, when I received your first letter. I don't say this to shame or to worry you, only to be honest. I miss you terribly. I miss our lives terribly. I miss who I was when you were here. Every day I wish the best for you, that you're able to rest and recover and be yourself again, György wrote. Every day, he missed Paul physically, the proximity of a body he'd loved so much. This he did not say. He did not admit to Paul the extent of his cravings and his hopeless attempts to scratch such an itch, in the sewers—we are speaking proverbially— and gutters and cesspits of New York, where, as though possessed by Paul's ghost, he replicated his beloved friend's role as centerpiece, as objet d'homme. He grew bold and propositioned men instead of waiting for them to drift his way. If he saw something he liked at the next urinal, he stared until it slipped back into its trousers or until it grew, aware of being watched, and solicited his assistance.

Of course, I was twenty-three, George told me, and even though nobody gets the chance, he said, to be twenty-three these days, to be twenty-three then and living underground was to have limitless demands. No, he would never take a wife. He would never grow a family. Not when all of this was in the world. Not when Paul was out there waiting to be healed, to rejoin him and be his companion, even if they were companions of a sort György had never heard of, never read about. He wanted, George told me, to be as unique as he felt.

===

The most important thing to avoid for me, Paul wrote, is the humiliation of being home. I don't only mean to be w/ my parents—but to be in this so-called city—this bloated, God-hungry, swampy slaughterhouse on the Mississippi. Who even was this "Saint" Louis? The saint of worthless conversations about the weather—no doubt.

My treatment has begun, & while I'm apprehensive I do feel optimistic—or at least there's a certain shadow of hope—that doctors do in fact know what they're doing. Someone has to, isn't that right? Let me know, when we see each other again, if I am happier. Perhaps I'll even finish that play. After I start it, anyway. Please imagine that I'm laughing as you read this, or the tone doesn't work at all.

I've never met this Noël Rivers, Paul went on (which was strange, George told me, because he *had* met Noël several times, and even though they disliked each other it seemed ridiculous to have been so uneventful that Paul could have forgotten), but you describe him aptly enough—he sounds sad, but in the way of sad people who refuse to realize they are sad. Perhaps one day he'll have what I had—a revelation as it were—& w/ his money be able to cloister himself in

one of those grand sanatoria in the mountains—w/ little villages &
chocolates & baskets of fruit, w/ alpine groves & rocky paths and so
on. Or perhaps he'll never realize it & just walk through life a horny
idiot—& would that be so terrible?

I'm lonely, too, friend. But then I was lonely in New York. I
don't mean that as a rebuke or indictment—just as an admission,
a confession. What I hope is to be nudged in the right direction—
shocked, as it were, back into place. My parents are deeply sup-
portive of the treatment, of course—even if they want me to do
something ridiculous once it's over, become a veterinarian or an
architect or something equally embarrassing. I just want to feel safe
around myself—something I imagine most people don't even have
to think about—something I'm sure you, György, have never had to
think about. I want to have my music & my books & my friends—
to look at paintings w/o feeling like I want to leap into them—&
to write or paint or take pictures of my own or sit there smoking like
a living sculpture, whatever it is I'm meant to do w/ this life—w/o
this constant gnawing in me like a rat biting into a live wire. I want
to be good, György. I want to be healthy. I want to want to live.

═══

Paul never came back to New York. Which now seems like no surprise but then seemed as shocking as the end of the world. And
it was, in a sense, the end of a world, a lovely world that felt as
secret, as remote, as the dark star where his ambitions had gone
to live. His letters, George told me—and I can attest, having seen
them myself, in Paul's script that transformed, over those weeks,
from microscopic and contained to loose, jagged, uneven, to drift-
ing up and over the lines on the paper like something seismic had

changed—were decreasingly coherent and full of strange gaps. Events he remembered changed their settings; what had happened on Paul's sofa was now György's. A conversation at Yvette's studio was now, as Paul told it, at the Waldorf. And these were the events Paul remembered at all. Admittedly, I'm confused lately, Paul wrote, so please forgive the inconsistentness of my writings. It's supposedly temporarily like everything else—the trembling + the chattering, par example—but I do feel improvements.

In one of the last letters György was to receive, Paul mentioned his love of the outdoors. I was an Eagle Scout! Someday, friend, I'll take you out for a camping trip + finally get you away from that big city + out camping out under the stars. It's like nothing else! You'll love it!

György would not be long in New York anyway—though he didn't know it then. In my mind, George told me, I was just about *there*. Making enough money to not only survive but to acquire— to buy his first painting, he said, and a beautiful new Olivetti, and a silver cigarette case he loved to pull out of his jacket pocket at parties. At Yvette's, he met not only writers and poets but the editors who worked with them, and who were interested in his ideas on film and its sociopolitical impact, as well as his small, slow-growing catalog of photographs. Even when he mentioned, in a tone that could have said *joke* if they wanted to hear it that way, the great leap forward in "the art of science fiction" that was *The Day the Earth Stood Still*, they did not laugh. They had read his little essay, they said, his little article, his little review, his little thoughts, in this or that little magazine or weekly, and they would have lunch and talk more, they said, once the busy season was behind them and they had a chance to get their bearings. *This is a very interesting politics you're developing, Mr. . . . . Kurtz, was it?*

I was positioned, George said, to have the right life.

In January of 1952, he was arrested. It was the loneliest time of all, George told me—Paul's letters had stopped and Yvette was teaching at some kind of retreat. The man in the subway toilet had been eager. Horrifically beautiful and a cock that took your breath away—even when it wasn't choking you, George confessed with a wheezy laugh. And tall, and blond, and handsome in all those mythic American ways. Succulent bait. He'd waited until he shot his load in György's mouth before he showed him his badge and produced the handcuffs. According to the cop, this young pervert had solicited him for sex—which of course he, an officer of the law, had declined. He was booked, charged, and released for his arraignment in two months. His name in the paper, there with all the other sex criminals.

It was either jail or deportation, Gil said as he took him out for a drink. "I'm sorry, good Georges. Perhaps, who knows, had you been more careful—but it's too late now." But how can one avoid a walking trap? George asked me. I refrained from pointing out the obvious, the monastic intent in Gil's suggestion.

Yvette, once she returned, was not only more sympathetic but more intelligent—and more prescient. "What are you going to do? Let them ruin your life? Absolutely not, Georgie—not a gem like you." All panics, Yvette said, die out or blow over. These people, she said, can't stay angry or sanctimonious forever. "Someday soon they'll forget all about the communists and the homosexuals and sink their teeth in some other poor bastard's neck. So until then— just go away. Go somewhere they don't know you, where they won't recognize you. Where they won't even be looking. Just go, Georgie. Go be someone else for a while."

He didn't want, he wrote to Paul, to get into the details, but he was leaving New York and on his way somewhere far, somewhere that barely exists. I hope you understand, he wrote, that I'm a desperate man, a man in love. I don't even know what I mean by love, just that I'm in it, and I want to see my closest, dearest friend before I disappear. I'll be in Saint Louis on the tenth of February—just passing through town, but with enough time for lunch, for a picnic, for a walk, for a long embrace, whatever you're able to give me. Since you haven't answered my recent letters I'm going to take a risk and look up your parents' address once I've arrived at the station. I will be careful, Paul—please don't worry. I will be discreet. We are friends who went to school together, that is all—how could they be angry about that?

There wasn't much he could bring, not on such short notice, and no one he could tell except Yvette—his only portal, George told me, to that other old life. He packed the Olivetti, his notebooks, his saved letters. He didn't want to risk stealing the Leica and left it behind. His photographs were too incriminating, especially with such charges on his record, and he gave them to Yvette, who kept them in a box on a shelf in her studio. Here Paul's image, his body, his spirit, sat shelved in the dark for years, George told me, until a pipe burst and flooded the studio and ruined much more, George told me, than a silly folder of old photographs, but ruined them all the same. There were no photos left, no poems, no drawings, and hardly anyone else to speak to; and, when he got to the train station where Yvette was waiting to say goodbye, nor was there Paul—not anymore. Right away, he could see she'd sobbed herself dry, and was at first touched by her sentimentality, by the idea that she would miss him so much. But she took his hand. She said, "I got the call before I walked over. Oh, Georgie, I'm so sorry. He loved you so much."

Las Vegas

THE GREAT PROBLEM OF TORTURE IS THE DEFINITION
of torture. Violence, as George reminded me, and who gets to define it. Because he was naïve, because he no longer had friends and
steeped himself in secrecy, because he was cautious and covered his
tracks, and above all because it was *medicinal*, in those days—and,
in many places, these—to torment a person therapeutically, it took
George Curtis several years to realize what had happened to the
person he'd loved most in the world. It wasn't until the clinic had
closed that the details of its program had entered the columns of
newspapers, and even then George had to read between the inky,
careless lines. It was unusual, one newspaper reported, in "this day
and age" to administer electroshock "unmodified"—that is, George
told me, without drugs. Patients are operated on while awake. They
experience their own convulsive paralysis. Which is to say Paul ex-
perienced it. He would have felt it annihilate him. And when it was
over, he'd have been taken back. He'd have been told it was up to
him now, these were *his* choices. His doctor would have promised
to help him. His doctor would have undressed him. You don't want

this to feel like love, the doctor said, do you? You don't want this to feel like pleasure, he'd have whispered in his ear. Whether Paul screamed, whether he was silent, George could not tell me, but he knew Paul had been dismantled and destroyed. He'd been turned against himself one so-called treatment at a time until there was no self to recognize. That this doctor was now "under investigation" cannot change what we know about life, George told me. And what we know, he said, is that a person's soul cannot go without recognizing itself, and in such circumstances it must depart. However you define it, George said, the kind and unforgettable stranger with a smile that'd changed one lonely orphan's entire life was tortured— to death—at the insistence, at the relief, of his own parents.

=

It was fear that brought Paul back, that reconjured Gil and Yvette, and the weather and the sour rain of New York, its brief, glorious flowerings and falls—his entire second life, to tell the truth, now that he was living his third—as they left Malibu and began the long climb from the beaches and the mountains to the speedway across the desert, to Las Vegas. He, too, could be tortured, even if the idea behind it, the philosophy and methodology, were quite different. Ostensibly, George had fallen for it again—the American man who traded blowjobs for entrapment, maybe blackmail. It wasn't yet clear what Jack was looking for but it was clear that he'd find it, and that George had compromised himself and was again vulnerable. He had no idea how long Madeline intended to hold them all hostage in Las Vegas, how long a "party" from someone so metastatically lonely could last. And after California, where else was there to go?

In the car, Jacques and Walt slept. Houghton thumbed
through a landscaping magazine. Madeline babbled with George
and Jack—Jack, who seemed extraordinarily interested in everything each of them said. You could almost see him taking notes,
George told me, raking their dead and idle chatter back and forth
for clues. He was no better at espionage than writing film scripts.
At least with film the only person's life he could ruin was his own.

It wasn't the first time George had been used. But it was *worse*,
he said, than what he'd felt four and a half years before; he felt *less*
prepared for it. At least the Dexedrine, George said, along with his
lack of sleep, excused the trembling and the sweating, the thun-
derous cloud of nervous energy that sat wedged between Houghton's indifference and Jack's patience. But even more than before
he felt the threat of prison or deportation, of returning to Budapest in a cage where some Soviet tormentor would read through
his papers and pull out his fingernails, gently peruse the marginalia of his books and with every treasonous thought tighten just
a little tighter—his stomach turning as he imagined it—the vise
in which they'd clamped parts of himself that might never again
feel the same. He saw Jack following or driving Ellman to some
agreed-upon place, a location Ellman finds exciting in its clandes-
tine glamour, its reek of the old days, the hopeful days. Whatever
drug it is and however Jack has administered it, it is beginning to
work; Ellman is beginning to realize his mistake. He sees the look
in Jack's eye. George had no idea what had passed between them,
what Ellman might have known or what truths he'd discovered,
nor why it was Jack who'd been sent, as George imagined, to erad-
icate him; but George saw all the same Jack's calm, his patience,
as Ellman drifts into pliancy, into helplessness. The tenderness of
those hands as they slide on a pair of gloves, as they wrap gently

around Ellman's own and lift the pistol to his mouth. And why couldn't that be George, before long? It was all too hideously easy to imagine, his life over because he'd let a man into it. Like so many of his kind, they'd say he died of careless affection, another mind lost to incurable sickness.

He closed his eyes and visualized his own heart and told it to slow itself, to calm itself. We haven't slept, he told his heart. Jack is no killer.

Their hotel was the tallest in Las Vegas, and Madeline had taken advantage of it with the full-floor penthouse. The room was nearly as large as her house in Malibu, and similarly furnished—brightly, desperately. Crossing the desert had taken the better part of the day and they only had time, Madeline warned, for a short nap before changing for dinner, and then the party would begin. She assigned them all their corners of the suite—she and Walt in one room, George and Jack in another, Jacques on one sofa, and Houghton on the other. Jack pretended to sleep. George didn't bother, and smoked as his heart thought of leaping from his body and crashing through the window. Nobody knew what they were doing here, nobody knew how many people would come. More ruinously, George did not know if he'd be able to escape this time, to untangle himself from whatever trap had snared him. *Who are you working for?* he wondered as he watched Jack breathe—not at all evenly, not at all deeply. His eyelids twitched but not in the way of dreams, only strain. Jack was trying, and despite everything it made George sad that a man so lovely and so admirable could be so mediocre, in need of such extensive critique and instruction, even in this. I realized then, George told me, that I was never meant to be around such people, such nothings—excepting Madeline, who really was one

of the greats. It hadn't been in my cards, he said, in the lines on
my palms, in the alignment of the planets, to get sent away from
New York. I was given a different life, he said, and the worst part
of me wasted it.

═══

Dinner was macabre. Victoria Munson joined them at the restaurant, a nondescript, unremarkable place that seemed suspiciously
beneath them all, until the food arrived. George was shocked.
"Our greatest kept secret," Victoria said, and giggled along with
Madeline at their ingenuity.

Victoria had brought with her a young woman, Elizabeth. She
didn't merit a last name, but merited, always, Victoria's "Isn't that
right?" or "Don't you think so?"—to which she nodded or smiled
or agreed. Unhitched from Victoria's side, she was rancid with
complaints. Her shoes hurt, the silverware was dull, her drink was
heavy on vermouth, someday she'd be taken seriously as a direc-
tress, she was still nauseated from the long drive through the desert, and why were there always so many men at these gatherings?
George smiled and she looked at him as if he were a roach or centi-
pede, something that'd scuttled into her space.

"I know, dear—isn't it awful?" Madeline offered Victoria's companion a cigarette. "But I do find that if you give them a chance,
you may discover they have more in common with you than you
think. In fact"—and here she laughed—"if there's an odd one out
at the table, it's certainly me." Jack frowned but she didn't see it.
"To me," she said, and toasted with her empty glass, "the one who
just doesn't belong."

"Madeline," Walt said.

"I wouldn't be so sure," Jack said.

"I would," Madeline said.

Victoria returned to the table and took up Elizabeth's hand. "I'm not sure what you're all discussing," she said, "but I think it should stop. It's rude to continue a conversation not everyone has followed from its beginnings." She brought that hand close to her; George could see her lips forming the creased closeness of a kiss; and then she caught herself and let go. "Tell me, dear Madeline—do you find that the drinks are stronger here than they used to be? Everyone seems in such a hurry these days to get tight, it's unconscionable."

Jacques nodded. "I think you're absolutely right, Miss Munson," he said.

"You've never been here."

"That's true."

"Can he even handle a drink? Why are there children here? Someone give him water. I don't want a scene."

A waiter took Jacques's martini away and replaced it with a glass of water, which he sipped reverently as if it were a gift. The salads arrived, their last course before dessert. No one seemed hungry enough to eat them, and shifted the lettuce back and forth on their plates as if combing a garden for a dropped earring. Madeline thanked them all for coming. "I know it was short notice, but you know how these things are. You have to seize the right moment. And what a moment!" She winked and raised her glass once more—still empty—and they all followed. George continued to rake and reorganize the leaves on his plate. Jack glanced at his watch. Houghton was looking around nervously for more alcohol. Elizabeth and Victoria held hands, staring morosely at their plates. Walt seemed half-asleep. In someone's ghost story, George thought, these same people were sitting around this same table, and he, too, was one of the dead.

"All right, everyone," Madeline said once they'd had their dessert and coffee. She hadn't yet stood, and so they, too, remained seated. "It's time we got started." She gestured to the waiter, who brought her purse and stood there waiting as she dug through it. "I knew I'd lose them," she muttered, and then laughed as she found whatever she'd lost. The waiter draped a napkin over his cupped hands. "Yes, it's time we got started." She counted out eight Dexedrines and reserved one for herself and dropped the other seven into the improvised basket. It was religious, George told me, the way they took them in silence and swallowed them one by one. Jack, the last one to receive, laughed and made the sign of the cross. Elizabeth, for whom it was already too late, began to sob and excused herself from the table.

THE TEST

Everything had been rearranged. The penthouse, once a stuffy refuge, was now gaudy with waitstaff and music, drinks, hors d'oeuvres, and little silver trays of cigarettes with matching matchbooks. The furniture had been reimagined for a dozen little conversations, all close enough to eavesdrop, and the terrace was available to the night despite the crackling chill that'd blown in with the sunset. Even the muslin over the doorways fluttered just so, as if it, too, had studied Madeline's instructions.

"You must let me have this room when you're not in town," Victoria said, and settled herself in the middle of the salon. She nearly pulled Elizabeth by the arm to convince her to join her.

Madeline laughed. "After tonight, you'll see why I'll never give up this room. You'll have to kill me for it."

"I haven't fought to the death in some time, Madeline, but if there's anyone I'd love to take up the challenge with me . . ."

George stepped out onto the terrace. Would it be too impulsive, too dramatic, to leap over the edge and be done with it? Before he could reach any conclusions, Jacques joined him. "I don't like these people anymore," he said.

"You just don't like them when Madeline is trying to impress someone unworthy of her."

"How do you know what I like and don't like?"

Another swish of the curtain. "And how are my two favorite fairies?" Jack said.

George stepped back against the railing and wrapped his fingers around his cigarette case. If he'd simply remembered it, if he'd carried it with him out of the room that morning, he wouldn't have known. He could've gone on feeling moony about Jack as long as he wanted, as long as it took to sweat it all out. "We were just remarking," George croaked, and coughed and tried again, "just remarking on how, if we had one more, we could protect a princess. And here we all are, the three fairies of Las Vegas."

Jack scoffed and spit over the railing. He was trying so hard. "There are two sissier ones inside," he said. "You'll have better luck with them, I imagine."

"Why is everyone out here?" Madeline demanded. "Get back inside at once. Nobody's to leave this room until at least ten of our guests have arrived." She frowned as they filed past her, back into the salon. George could tell the Dex was beginning to hit the rest of them; they were getting twitchy and quick, glancing like birds or rats. They sat around a coffee table and stood up again. Walt neatened his trousers as if conducting surgery. Victoria lit another cigarette before finishing her first. Then the door opened and in flooded a gush of guests, all chattering as their elevator conversations came to a close. Thank God, George thought, and signaled for a drink.

=====

Conversations:

Why shouldn't we have the freedom to fly or display the swastika? It was only a symbol, a memory of the great ambitions of a country. Yes, the Germans got sidetracked—derailed, as it were, if you'll excuse the metaphor, which only occurs to me now as perhaps inappropriate, haha. But you see what I mean, don't you? Let me ask you this: What do the stars and stripes symbolize? Agreement, analysis, logic, conclusions and such—time spent, as it were, and often time wasted. But the swastika? Action. *Force.* They saw what they wanted and they took it, they knew what would make them great. Surely you can understand that? If you ask me, a lot of people find it inspirational, even uplifting. They're just afraid to say so—cowed as they are by today's liberal intolerance. One used to be able to have a real *discussion.*

It was unimaginable, simply unimaginable, to use a black olive in place of a green olive. Really there should be two words, one of them an olive and one of them something else, something *not* olive. Victoria, you must listen to this—this poor girl asked if it wouldn't be possible to use a black olive in a martini. A *black* olive. Have you ever heard such a thing?

Hungary? Hungary's already passé, my friend. This week, it's all Suez. Nobody remembers Hungary anymore.

By then, Aunt Jane was no longer quite in her right mind, if you know what I mean. We were having breakfast and it was one of her good days, and she turned to me and said, "I can't wait to meet Jesus." I said that's very nice, Jane, but then she said, "And God. I can't wait to meet God and Jesus. I'd like to go now. Right now." She was smiling and I didn't know whether to laugh or call the police. And then she kept living and living, you know. God bless her, I suppose.

To be interesting? *That* is the myth, or at least its virtue is mythical. You have all these people running around calling things interesting. Oh, isn't this interesting? Isn't that? Well, what *else* is it? So it has your interest—and what's so special about you?

Oh, those old bombs were so *simple*. Not to mention there wasn't enough U-235 or fissile plutonium buried out here to wage even the daintiest all-out nuclear war. The Japanese are lucky our early attempts were so feeble. No, these days we're able to maximize even *depleted* uranium and construct something unimaginably more powerful with isotopic deuterium and tritium. How much more? A thousand times the strength of the Hiroshima bomb— and I say this conservatively. I suppose I shouldn't be talking about this, but it's not as if anyone could duplicate the design—it's like a symphony or a ballet, the way it comes together. I do wish it were easier to communicate the sheer beauty of it.

If you ask me, this vogue about the foreign films is only a work-around for bad acting. Of course you can give a phenomenal performance if nobody *really* understands you. It's just like in the twenties when they let in all that sound, or even now, trying to dazzle us with all these vulgar dyes on the film itself—suddenly you have this *distraction*.

If only there were a way to tell you, to even articulate what chronic pain is like. Nobody believes me! And then you start thinking of extremes, of these desperate, psychotic lengths. I was getting a massage—this is an example, mind you—and he said, "Madame, is there anything in particular you would like me to pay attention to today?" And I said—and I said this before I could stop myself, it just flew right out of my mouth—I said, "Please just grab that chair and break it over my back." I was mortified but this is how it is, do you understand? You get so desperate for a cure that you imagine crawling into a meat grinder, or having an especially sturdy lad hold you by the ankles over a balcony and shake you out like an old rug. Say, do you have your golf clubs with you? Would you like to beat me therapeutically? [Delayed laughter] You see? This is what I mean. No one can help me.

Don't be silly. Of *course* Walt could trust Ronald Reagan.

Masterpieces? Who needs them. Masterpieces are for people in their twenties. Give me an *oeuvre* or nothing.

He was horrible, absolutely horrible. He said such embarrassing things. At one party he said, "And now for my next trick, ladies and gentlemen, I will make this drink disappear," and then he drank the drink. Nobody laughed but him. He spent an hour in the bathroom while everyone waited. I think he was crying but he never told me the truth. Absolutely horrible. You know me, I'd never say anything as evil as to express gratitude over one's passing, but in this case . . . well, no, I'd never say it, never. How terrible it must be to be dead! But he does seem happier.

All this sweetness, this innocence and indulgence. The pies and the cakes and the syrups, it's all so disgusting. If you think about it, really think about it, the relationship between slavery and sugar is the *core*, the very heart, of American hypocrisy.

Marvelous. I've always wanted to meet an artist. I was beginning to assume they weren't real.

Maldonado—doesn't that mean "bad gift"?

You never forget the stench of it, if you want to know the truth. All those people.

Nobody believes it when I tell them, but that's how she makes her living. Just taking pictures of strangers in the street.

In a way, the concentration camp is a form or a frame. It needs *something* to fill it, yes? So of course it's aesthetic—it demands a constant influx of material, or content, to meet the demands of its artistic medium. If you must, you could say it reached its apotheosis—is that too offensive?—with Auschwitz, the perfect concentration camp, the *Ulysses* or Proust, the *Parsifal* of camps. But of course, unfortunately for the Jews, and I suppose the fairies and congenital idiots and whoever else, they required a specific kind of content. It wasn't like with poems, per se, where you just write down words—no sir. It was so much more than poetry.

———

Despite everything, George told me, it wasn't a terrible party. In fact, with a few drinks and a second Dexedrine, he began to have a pleasant time, a time he imagined he'd remember fondly in some years. He maintained his distance from Jack, who was either drunk or giving a good performance of it as he laughed stupidly with people he'd only just met, maybe getting them to say something he'd help them regret.

By now, the suite was incomprehensibly packed—so full that George wondered, in brief waves of paranoia, if they hadn't made the hotel top-heavy. There was so much traffic and cigarette smoke and bumping into strangers that they'd begun, as the hours accumulated, to develop traffic patterns. As if it were a rule, they stepped out onto the balcony through the door to the right, and stepped back inside through the door adjacent. People began to skirt clockwise around the discussion circles Madeline had arranged, and they exchanged, with help from the waitstaff, their empty glasses for full ones only on the move. You always had a stubborn one to fuck it all up, George told me, and he left that person's identity up to my imagination—though I didn't need much help. Nobody knew then that Victoria was seriously ill. It wasn't the sort of thing she'd want people to know about her. But it did affect her mobility, and she didn't see much point, she said, in walking all the way over *there*—she pointed—just to speak to a charming young woman who's right *here*. The woman, upon hearing this, disappeared, and Victoria beckoned Elizabeth in her stead—who swam against the current of bodies and knocked over drinks and extinguished cigarettes—only to unleash a psalm book of bitterness. George laughed and walked away. It was something he'd have to remember for a film, if he ever went back to writing them.

Generally, the party was like that—a great mine of strangeness, of striking details. Most of Madeline's parties were like this, but this was by far her greatest achievement, her great curio, she'd have called it, of mysteries—actors and directors, museum curators, a ceramics artist who had at last, she said, begun to be taken seriously. A choreographer and the tobacco executive she'd married. Various species of painters (none of whom George had heard of). A lounge singer who kept trying to sing but whom people asked to step away, please, he was frightfully loud. An unusual percentage of accountants Madeline could not explain—"I swear to you, George, I knew nothing"—and their confused, trembling husbands and wives who'd never seen such a crowd. One child, who said very little and played with matches while people watched.

There was a man who seemed to be a nuclear physicist or a very good impersonation of one, and whose love of idle chatter might have been treason. A professor of English poetry. A professor of German poetry. Two linguists who never agreed with each other unless it was against someone else in the room, and only then if it were something ostensibly simple or obvious. There was the woman who kept asking the linguists their favorite words as a pretense to get them to fight, once they'd at last settled down. A professor of French poetry. A professor of French philosophy. A small, roving pack of pugs that wheezed and gagged in joy. The young man who died (it wouldn't be until morning that they discovered him), with no identifying papers or unique possessions, at least not in his pockets. Several mathematicians, whose general disgust everyone found delightful. A man who'd been a monk and a woman who'd been a nun, neither of whom ever quite got around to talking to the other. Too many poets to count, and four playwrights—an apocalypse of playwrights, as someone said. A practicing philosopher, whose general disgust was terrifying. A schoolteacher—this is what everyone called her, as if she were in some lost western town. What is it that you *do?*—this is how everything started, how they all found out about one another. This is James, a pilot. This is Heloise, a chemist. This is Charlotte, a keeper of bees. This is Alistair, the last living member of the Whigs. Everyone, George said with a smile, was just so interesting.

It reminded him, he told me, of New York. A decade ago he'd wandered similar parties full of a similar variety of professions and the people attached to them like shadows, though people didn't smile so much then. Those rooms—artists' lofts, sweaty galleries, moldy and urine-tinged taverns—hadn't been such smoky seas of malevolent teeth. I feel, he imagined himself writing to Yvette, I feel as if I've stepped into a parallel dimension, living again this old life but not quite the same life. Perhaps, George told me, he'd been banished for a reason, that this other dimension was where he *really* belonged, among these not-talented-enoughs, not-brilliant-enoughs. In New York, he said, he'd been training for something truly great, and perhaps it'd been beyond him, perhaps the universe had simply said no and put him here instead. Nobody here, he would write in this unsendable letter, will ever amount to anything, nobody here will be remembered—and I do include myself, George Curtis, whom history will forget. Perhaps only Madeline, he'd say. You remember her—Madeline Morrison—or at least you remember how I talked about her, all those years ago. They'll never forget who she was, who she'd been. But to be in a room with you, Yvette, and Gil and Hal—how could I have been so stupid? He'd thrown everything away, George, and on something as lousy as one more beautiful dick. There would always be more dicks. There would never be another Yvette.

He made his way toward the balcony.

"Oh, it's you," someone said.

"It's me."

They smiled and looked elsewhere, a place that wasn't in the room. Then they took a breath and recited, "We only have five minutes to save the earth!"

"Then we'd better not waste any more time," George said, and excused himself and followed the flow of bodies outside. He stood alone in a tiny corner he made for himself, clutching his drink and his cigarette like scepter and orb. Again, the faraway pavement called his name, the shimmering city below. It would be a scene, of course, but would Madeline mind? A suicide at a party—of course such things were riveting, but it would ruin

her plans, whatever they were. She continued to distribute Dexedrine as if it were an hors d'oeuvre, and George had overheard her
whispering, with Heloise the chemist, about lysergic acid diethyl-
amide. Every time someone tried to leave, she intervened—"You
absolutely don't want to miss this, you'll never forgive yourself,
believe me." For George to leap over the railing and get the police
involved and put people out of the mood—she'd never forgive
him, even if he were just crunched-up splattered garbage for the
gutter. Tomorrow, he thought. Tomorrow we can take care of
this little problem and be on our way. Tomorrow, Jack will have
no one left to spy on, Madeline will lose a great weight from her
life, and Jacques will be free of the sad shadow he'd caught like an
infection. *George*, whispered the great height, and George said,
out loud, "Tomorrow," and flicked his cigarette over the rail and
followed the traffic back inside.

===

Such things can always wait one more day. If you're lucky, you always find a reason, someone who loves you, something to need
you, one more cigarette or long walk or glance around a favorite
corner. When my children are grown, people say. When I've written my book, when the last person who wishes me a good morning
forgets—that will be my time. And the time does not arrive—for
most people. For many it does. You would think, George told me,
that it's the people who lose sight of the future, for whom their
forthcoming lives drown in darkness, but it's not that at all. It's
those who know. Those who see. Time into space—that's what it is,
he said. The future and the past snap back into a single dimension,

the flattened present. All of life, right there in front of you like the walls of a cell. All at once there's forever nowhere left to go.

It must have been two or three in the morning. No one seemed interested in knowing. The occasional guest had fallen asleep but most continued to chatter and shriek and clink their glasses together and sputter with drink as they laughed; Madeline kept them generously drugged. Where had she obtained so much of it? George wondered. What kind of doctor had she swindled or sweet-talked or blackmailed? It was a great cardiac emergency of a party, and reeked bitterly of sweat. They were having the time of their lives.

When they found themselves together, alone on an ottoman surrounded by others too delirious to follow a conversation, Madeline took his hand and said to him, "George," and brought his knuckles to her cheek, her lips. She was drunker than she meant to be, and sensual about it. Perhaps he was, too, and hadn't noticed. "I'm so glad you've come to live with me. Or that I kidnapped you, however we should tell it. I'd say it's all very *Sunset Boulevard* but that would mean—"

"You're shockingly beautiful, Madeline."

"Yes, yes, that's exactly it."

It was only that morning—or yesterday morning, if you went by the clock—that he was in that room, stashed away in Madeline's house. He'd sat awake through the night, as he would again this night, and considered his life and his work as separate if not parallel threads, two aspects of himself to manage. Hundreds of miles away, his ideas and papers and his work scattered across "his" desk, accumulating in "his" workspace, while servants he didn't pay brought him food he hadn't made, wine he hadn't bought or even opened. Here, in his hand, a martini he hadn't mixed or even thought of, just accepted. It was so easy, George told me, to let them collect you like this, to let them carry you around or show you off. Even the room she'd given him was nothing but glass: Look at my writer. And what had he done about it? He'd written. He'd performed. She was, as she'd said, so proud.

"I remember the first time I ever saw you," George told her. He'd overturned her grip and now held her, directed her. "I was young. Very young. I had met someone very rich who bought me clothes and who showed me the parts of the city I had never been able to see. His name was Noël, with two little dots like I'd once had." In fact, George went on, Noël had pointed this out not long after they met, to look for artists together. Noël had dots and György had his. Wasn't it fate? George had never found the strength or cruelty to point out that Noël's diacritics were only similar in appearance, and even then by accident. You see, he told Madeline, whose eyes were quaking in her head—she was utterly spellbound—you see, what Noël Rivers had, in his given name, was a dieresis. "It signals to the reader that a vowel is pronounced separately, not combined with its neighbor. It is adjacent but apart," he told Madeline, who shivered with revelation. "But in György—did you know I was called György?—it's not only a different mark, an umlaut, but an inaccurate umlaut. They aren't even supposed to be dots, Madeline. It was just that your alphabet failed. I know it's not your fault, but it's a fact." What György had lost the moment he'd left home were the marks unique to his language, and even though the language had come with him, its alphabet had, at least in part, been left behind. "You see, it's supposed to be like this," he told Madeline, and uncurled her palm in his lap. He traced, softly, the letters of his

real name, and above the o drew not the two dots of an umlaut or
misplaced dieresis but two subtle diagonals, someone's lazy twin
apostrophes. "That's how it should be," he said, and closed her
palm so she could keep it.

"I've gotten lost," he said, and laughed as he reached for a tray
of cigarettes. "I was telling a story, not giving a lecture." He was
young, he repeated, and he'd met this Noël who employed him,
and they went to see an early production of *Streetcar*. Noël had
known Tom for years and enjoyed the transparency of his plays,
how he was there in every line, a little glow in every character, but
for George it was a first—he was transfixed and in awe, and a little
terrified. "You were so radiant," he told Madeline. "So tragically
magnetic, so ethereal. Were it not for your skill, nobody would
have believed you were she, because she is worn and tired and you
were . . ." He smiled. Flakes of ash fell as she wiped a tear from the
corner of her eye, and she laughed at herself, her feelings. But they
were wonderful feelings. "It was the real thing, Madeline. You are
the real thing. After all, they used to say I had an eye for it. Noël
hired me to be his eye, you know. And you did it all yourself. You
built yourself. Do you understand?"

For a moment, George wondered if he hadn't made a mistake—
if this wasn't too much for her and she'd make her own scene, ruin
her own party. She was breathing fast and shaking so badly he
gently took the cigarette from her fingers and gave it to an ash-
tray. But then it happened: she closed her eyes, went completely
still, and let her shoulders drape down her back like wings ruffled
back into place. She opened her eyes; the feelings were gone. "Oh,
George"—she laughed, much louder than before—"you always
know just what to say. Thank you, truly. You're such a dear friend
and I'd simply die without you." She kissed him on the cheek.

"I've said it a million times, but thank you so much for coming. I can't wait to see what you think of our little surprise. Say"—she stretched her hand out into the crowd—"have you met Charlotte?"

He had not.

"This is Charlotte, a keeper of bees. Excuse me."

Charlotte smiled. "An apiarist, yes. And you are?" Her hand hovered between them, which he took and kissed gently, all part of the agreement.

"George," he said.

"And what do you do, George?"

A circulator of blood. A sort of fancy respirator. Like many, he might have told Charlotte, I transform oxygen and nutrients into carbon dioxide and fertilizer. I breathe and eat and drink and piss and shit and sweat. I ejaculate into men's bodies and they ejaculate into mine. I experience feelings—often too many—and wonder, *Isn't it possible to experience fewer feelings? Different feelings?* "I work on scripts," he said. "It's not terribly exciting."

"Not exciting!" she said. "Well, tell me this—how thrilling is it, do you think, to work with bees? Bees, Mr. . . . your name again?"

"Dieresis."

"Mr. Dieresis. What a lovely name."

═══

Some people want nothing more than to be haunted. They look for ghosts and devils, for spirits to possess them. Are they vacant? A soul's container without the soul like a pitless peach? Not necessarily, George speculated, only lonely for themselves. They long to be, as one philosopher put it, the partners of their own thoughts, but don't quite know it. Their souls lie hidden or camouflaged and they take this for abandonment, and so share themselves, their spiritual bereavement, with obsessions. So much can fit into one human heart. Each of us can be, if we get lost, a little ark of vast demons ferried from life to life. And sometimes we drift, George told me, into sudden storms of shipwrecked lives, roomfuls of neurotics unburdening themselves of their hauntings.

The last George had heard of Jacques while he was alive—or Jake Belami, as he came to be known—he'd just gotten involved with a production company that made "athletic films" about Greek and Roman wrestling. You get the idea, he told me. There were underground films, too, ones they couldn't sell through the mail, but films Jacques made nonetheless, and even though he never saw one of them, George knew what would make them successful, the limits to which Jacques was capable of going, in fact enthusiastic to go to. But there was some mix-up, George found out later, or betrayal or double cross or deal gone bad—you know how these things are, he said. It was still very murky and you couldn't rely on the newspapers to tell it right, and maybe one day they'd untangle it, one day Jacques would see justice, but for the time being no one knew why he'd been strangled and left to float in a pool.

The details of Victoria Munson's death in 1957 are far less murky and private, even if there was, all the same, a scandal to bury. It wasn't the cancer that got her after all. In those days, George said, Mulholland Drive was quite the killer, and when they arrived on the scene—when the police found her and the girl who'd been driving—there were some who couldn't even look. It was as if, one said, they'd fused with the convertible itself. But who was the girl? This is what everyone wanted to know. Who was she, and why had she been driving Miss Munson's expensive car in lieu of the chauffeur? Simply a distant cousin, the family said, in town from Ohio, and who better to entertain her than a legendary actress? Victoria and Elizabeth weren't related of course, but nobody chased it. It was never as exciting when they were women. Not unless they were mothers. It was mothers and men they wanted to ruin, otherwise it was just two girls keeping each other company. They had to burn her, George said. One has to assume their ashes were blended forever, not to mention peppered with various steels and irons and magnesiums, whatever it was they put into automobiles in those days.

Houghton, of course, did die of cancer, but not before a dozen operations on his neck that left him voiceless and unable to eat, and so physically changed he was no longer recognizable as the actor he'd been, just an old man waiting to be pushed, in his wheelchair, from one window to another. It became difficult for him to hold his head erect and he took on the stoop of a waterfowl looking for prey, or just watching its own reflection. When George read about his death in the paper, he was astonished by the man's accomplishments, all the films he'd worked on and foundations he'd started, not to mention his little cheese shop in Malibu where, the obituary said, he brought joy, culture, and the sophisticated, sumptuous tastes of Paris to a little seaside village in California. The last time George had seen him, all Houghton had been able to think about were his failures, his wasted life.

Not long after that party, Walt was blacklisted. At first George assumed it had been Jack who reported him, who provided some dossier, but later it became clear it couldn't have been Jack, not by any means. Really, it could have been anyone, any of the young men he'd taken and dropped over the years, any of the actresses who hadn't liked working with him but knew his secrets, or just

a film producer who'd regretted paying so much for one mediocre performance. At first, George said, they say he enjoyed his
retirement—he was sailing, eating, traveling. He took up watercolors (they were awful) and would write his memoirs. He bought
a cabin near Idyllwild and a bungalow in Palm Springs and shuffled between them like a migratory bird, and only returned to Los
Angeles when Madeline needed him like she needed a certain fur
or necklace, the right accessory for a public appearance. He went
out less and less and began to rely on hustlers, young men he met
down in the valley who knew other men to send up the mountain.
Eventually—they used the word *inevitably* in the paper, George
told me—he was robbed. There wasn't even much cash in the safe,
and it was hard to know whether or not this was why they beat
him, why they were so brutal. He did live, but with that crushed
and asymmetric face and without the use of his legs, not for much
longer. It wasn't something he was willing to take, not with who
he'd been.

That is the past, of course. Rooms and rooms of the chattering
dead whose confinement to extinction hasn't saved them, George
told me. They are still looking for their souls or something to
simulate them. "Are you listening?" he asked—in my view rather
suddenly, even uncharacteristically. We were in the front room of
the apartment, where we usually had these conversations. A polite
phrase of Schumann was murmuring on the radio and the windows were drawn open and the city lived without us, people eating and smoking and ringing the little bells on their bicycles and
talking about work, about love, about music—all this four flights
down. "Of course I'm listening, George," I told him, and put my
hand to his cheek. He felt a mottled sort of hot and cold, like a dinner poorly microwaved, and he laughed at my nervousness. I was

always so tender, as he'd once told me. "No," he said, "I meant are you listening to Madeline? Are you listening to Jack and Jacques? They aren't finished with us." At least they certainly weren't finished with him, George, the one who'd been there and who still knew their voices, their obsessions. He had seen their souls and it was his great error, he said, not to help them meet again, to become the companions they'd always needed and whose absence had killed them all.

—————

People were beginning their end:

Like Los Angeles in the rain, their little patterns of traffic slowed to a sluggish, sad crawl—if they even bothered to step outside. Many had rooted themselves in chairs or were leaning against walls as they spoke, and their voices were quieter now; no one seemed invested in being heard, only acknowledged as having spoken. Yet few were asleep or even drowsy—the drug had done its job. George could see them considering the details, the density of cigarette smoke, the fingerprints on the windowglass, the way one of the lamps flickered if you bumped into it, the suede of the sofas, the rainbow slick of brine in the empty glasses as the waitstaff took them away. Whereas before they showered the room around them with sparks and blinded themselves with their own light, they now sat like undisturbed candles and waited. They were ready, as Madeline had planned, to see.

Victoria and Elizabeth had suffered some sort of argument— certainly not the kind they'd want anyone to decode, even if George could read it. Between sips from her martini and drags on her cigarette, Victoria told stories about the old days no one

wanted to hear—again—and paused every now and then to re-
flect, as if none of them were there, how her life had been finished
for so long, how she'd hung around like a stray, unwanted dog,
that she should have killed herself years ago, driven over a bridge,
slit her wrists in the bathtub. And then she'd say, of one of the
great directors, "He was always taking a little sniff, like this"—she
demonstrated—"from a little ring he wore on his pointer finger. It
was cocaine that made those pictures so great, didn't you know?"
Elizabeth, meanwhile, was refusing to leave the balcony. Perhaps it
was calling to her the way it'd called to George. He was, he told me,
embarrassed by how eager he was to sit and watch. They'd have to
drag her inside, Elizabeth threatened, and when no one reached
for her she flicked her cigarette over the edge and came back into
the salon, where Victoria chastely took her hand and called her a
sweet and stupid girl, a girl who had so much to live for, unlike the
actual living dead, she said, "as some of us have become."

A man who'd been to Spain in his youth had stripped to the
waist and begun twirling his jacket like a matador, though because
he was British he insisted on translating. "Bull!" he shouted as
people laughed and stepped away from him. "Bull!" In a failed pir-
ouette, he fell forward and landed on a glass someone had left next
to a sofa. His bloody arm lay across his lap as if he'd been gored.
"There is no future, is there?" he asked a much younger man, who
ignored him. "Yes, yes, it's all getting very dark now." Calmly, he
stood and wrapped his shirt around the wound and signaled for
another drink.

Someone had gone downstairs and won an appalling amount
of money, which she apparently didn't need. It was everywhere,
like cigarette butts outside a movie theater. They found it on glass
tabletops and rolled the bills into straws, though there wasn't

much of anything to snort. It stuck sweatily to elbows and forearms and scuttled across the floor by the open doorways to the terrace. Naturally, not all of Madeline's invitees were as indifferent to money as the woman who'd won it, and little by little when no one seemed to be looking the money simply disappeared, which may have been, some said, the woman's magic trick all along. "Enjoy," she said to people, seemingly at random, but they always blushed and turned away.

Houghton was a failure—at least in his own narrative, though it wasn't so easy to take him seriously. He was better at acting—in fact better at selling cheese, George said—than he was at being consoled. No one wanted his laments, and if they were patient they quickly disappointed him with an insufficient pity, or simply a pity he felt was in the wrong register. It wasn't that he disliked his films—in fact he was quite proud of them, and frankly he found it troubling that someone he spoke to in great need, in *great vulnerability*, Houghton said, would so casually dismiss them as tripe, even if he *had*, admittedly, in his moment of weakness, called them tripe. Of course they weren't tripe; he was just vulnerable, he was just upset—how was that not obvious? It was a fugue, George said, and as they approached the last and loneliest hours of the night it only crescendoed. "I thought I would change the world," he told one woman, and when she touched his cheek and said, "No one changes the world," he stepped away from her like she'd called him something obscene. He'd have slapped her, George said, had the waitstaff not intervened with their suggestions—a cigarette, sir? An hors d'oeuvre?—and given her a chance to escape.

The carpets were stained, the tile sticky. None of the furniture—at least not the upholstery—would survive. One sofa sat covered in cigarette burns, too many for it to seem accidental. They tried to hide it, but several of the men had agreed there was no longer any point in waiting for the restroom when the terrace was open to the city below. Which was also available for those who had drunk too much or too quickly, and who shielded their faces from view as though they were just taking some air as they convulsed in their imagined solitude. If anyone was below, George remembered thinking, they'd hardly have been surprised by this city's unique offering of rain. Not many people walked a city's streets, even Las Vegas, at three or four in the morning, and if you did, you probably weren't going to tell anyone what had befallen you.

One of the professors—George couldn't remember what he taught or studied—had somehow got hold of a half dozen topographical maps, which he unrolled onto an ashen and liquor-dampened coffee table and examined with great, careful interest. Jack, too, watched with interest, standing behind this cartographically inclined professor, though he didn't appear to recognize any of the locales, George told me, and frowned in a frustration it was hard not to enjoy, even to relish. Before long, the professor had a small audience who stood in a half-moon at his back. All were silent as he traced his fingers over the landscape, as he pointed to one mountain and another, a riverbed, a large, open basin of nothingness. George had never seen so many people stand so reverently, not even in religious gatherings. They were entranced, he said. They'd been bewitched.

His own mind—that, too, had been bewitched, he knew this. Though it wasn't so easy, any longer, to give these people the attention they sought, at least in this setting. He hadn't slept since Tuesday and what once felt like a superpower was slowly becoming a curse; he wondered what he was doing, why he'd chosen this. Not long ago he'd been safe, he'd been forgotten. It doesn't take much to undo oneself but it does take discipline to remain undone and George had grown weak, lonely. And not only that, he'd become, with one man, exactly what he'd escaped—a sort of property of the state. He just didn't know what state. A resinous gin swirled in his glass, no longer worth drinking but something to carry around, an object to ward off more spirits, as it were, and he smiled at his own silent joke. Across the room, a woman smiled back. *Are you thinking of taking a wife, in the next few years?* Noël's voice splashed into his head like a drink poured too greedily, and George felt guilty for it. One smile, he thought, and she becomes your accessory? Your shield? It was what they wanted, whoever *they* were. You know what I mean, he told me, and I did. I still do.

"Does anyone else think we've been lured up here to be killed?" a poet speculated. It came at the wrong time, an arrow fired with a little bump to the elbow that hit no one. Though perhaps they did consider it, sipping from their glasses, pulling from their cigarettes, grinding their teeth, scratching at their forearms, cracking their knuckles, itching with sweat and attention, swaying like wheatgrass; perhaps they pictured the gas from the vents or the poison in the hors d'oeuvres or the sudden, mutual agreement to leap from the city's highest balcony, but no one answered him, this poet, and he left the circle that seemed to have rejected him. He had a name, surely, but no one knew it, and as I mentioned before, there were no identifying papers.

===

Like they'd come to roost before dawn, people began to gather around Madeline at the center of the suite. On the arms of sofas they perched; at the stained, crumb-covered rug they scratched with their nervous little talons. It was perhaps five in the morning, couldn't have been much later—in the mountains there was still nothing of a glow, nothing of a purpling. Conspicuously—George used this word, and I could tell he'd thought about it, he'd looked for it—conspicuously, Walt sat directly to Madeline's right, and held her hand as she said thank you, as she said you are too kind, I'm so glad you all could come, we still have something for you, something you can't get anywhere else in the world, no matter how hard you try. It should have frightened them out of the room but they were enchanted and could not move. A stillness had arrived and held them like silver gelatin, this great engineered moment in time. People talked about that night, George told me, for the rest of their lives.

Victoria lay sunken in the chair she'd chosen. "We're waiting until the sun comes up, is that it? So we all have to look at each other, Madeline?"

"You say that as if you're my hostage."

"You know I'm just curious. I like to *know*, you know?"

"To know," echoed the practicing philosopher.

Houghton crawled out of his despair and said, "I heard once that some man named Hugh—yes, a David Hugh—postulated long ago that we never truly know if the sun—"

"Hume."

Houghton glared at the philosopher and said, "Pardon me, sir," and continued as he turned his gaze back to Madeline: "This David Hugh postulated that the sun is only an assumed repetition, that we don't know for a fact that the sun will even rise. Isn't that fascinating? I believe it was a deduction."

"Induction."

"No, no, that wasn't it, I'm sure of it."

"Excuse me." The philosopher stood and walked out onto the

balcony. George waited for a scream or the rustle of clothing but there was nothing.

"Imagine," said Jack, "the sun never coming back up. What horseshit."

"I've had nightmares about that," Jacques said.

"Who is this child? Madeline, shouldn't he be in bed?"

Walt laughed. "I assure you, Miss Munson, Jacques is a grown man."

"Ah, so your tastes are maturing?"

George cleared his throat and asked, "What were your nightmares? What happened in them?"

Madeline nodded at Jacques, and Walt touched him on the elbow. Presumably he'd never spoken in front of so many people; presumably, George told me, no one had ever asked him what he thought about anything. His voice quavered as he said, "We were in our old house"—and didn't describe it—"and Ma was washing the dishes. It was after dinner. Then the power goes out—like it would during a thunderstorm?—and she reaches for the flashlight we keep by the back door, but it's dead. She tries other batteries but they're dead, too, nothing works. So we go out and it's a clear sky, a starry night. But then the stars start disappearing, they go out one at a time like the little bulbs on signs, you know? And I start crying," Jacques said, and it seemed as if he would cry now, and George regretted asking him, regretted risking such vulnerability in someone so wounded, "because I know what it means."

"This is so embarrassing," Elizabeth said to her benefactress. "Please tell me nobody knows we're here."

"I think it's fascinating," Houghton said.

A voice came from the balcony: "You think there's an eighteenth-century philosopher named Hugh who wrote about deduction."

Houghton laughed. "I may not be an expert or a man of great study, but I'm quite sure Mr. Hugh wrote about *in*duction."

"You all are so horrible," someone said, and she laughed as she added, "it's marvelous."

"You know, I was feeling quite wonderful a moment ago—and I refuse to lose that. I'm *still* feeling quite wonderful, and none of you are going to take that away from me, not tonight."

"It's morning, Charlotte dear."

"It is certainly not. I simply don't do mornings."

"Then you don't have much time."

Walt shrugged. "None of us have much time."

"Now *that's* a fact." Victoria sputtered her diesel laugh. "Yes, and what a fact that is."

"Are you going to let poor Jacques finish his story?" Madeline asked.

Elizabeth snorted. "Why should we? The child is describing a dream. We all have dreams. Dreams aren't real, and they never make any sense or mean anything."

"He's nearly your age," Walt said.

"And I'm a sweet little baby."

"Have you read Freud, Miss . . . ?" someone asked, a bit sickly— likely one of the painters.

"Of course I've read Freud."

"Miss . . . ?"

"Don't mind her," Victoria said. "A little too much sun on Catalina recently. She's all overheated."

"We were just on Catalina, too," Jack said. "That fancy sailing club, right? The place with all the crab?"

"The place with all the crab," someone echoed. "Perfectly iambic, daresay Shakespearean."

Charlotte leaned forward and gathered what remained of her charm. "Mr. Dieresis, do you enjoy Shakespeare?"

George pretended he hadn't heard.

"The hell with traditions anyway," Jack said. "The hell with the past."

"But Jack," Madeline said. "The past is all there is." She laughed and gestured across the room, as though she'd provided all these people as evidence. "All is a shared past. What's really done with, what's really over, is the future. There is no future."

"You're out of your mind."

"She's quite right," Victoria lamented. "There hasn't been a future in decades."

"Life on Earth is meaningless," someone said. "Always has been, I'm afraid, but here we are, and we go on."

"No, thank you."

"No?"

"I'm not interested."

"In what?"

"There hasn't been a future since 1945," Walt said. "We have it. The Russians have it." He shivered in his seat and squeezed Madeline's hand. "With that cloud hanging over our heads? How could there be anything after?"

"So, what, you just give up, then?"

"We've already given up. We're already dead. You're dead. Everyone here is dead."

But Charlotte hadn't given up. "Excuse me, Mr. Dieresis—do you enjoy the plays of Shakespeare?"

"Perhaps you've confused him with Dr. Umlaut, Charlotte dear."

"Oh, is Umlaut here? I thought he was still in Zurich."

"He told me his name was Dieresis—perhaps I'm not saying it correctly?"

"His name is Curtis. Perhaps he was joking?"

"Yes. Joking."

"I'm sorry, Charlotte," George said.

She wouldn't look at him, and waved her hand for another drink. The waitstaff didn't respond, and when nothing arrived she began to look around as though she'd lost a diamond or forgotten who she was.

"I have something special planned, Charlotte," Madeline said. "Gin will only interfere."

"What does gin matter to the dead."

"Out with it, Madeline." Victoria clapped her hands. "Enough with this suspense."

Walt showed Madeline his watch. She considered it. They were approaching 5:20, according to George's own watch—he remembered quite well, he told me. In fact, he said, if he closed his eyes the numbers seemed burned somewhere inside him. Not the backs of his eyelids, he said, it wasn't like that at all. It was as if, with nothing else to guard it, his vision grew vulnerable and something came after it, like a creature that attacked only in dreams. He closed his eyes. *Yes, there they are.* It was then, he said, that Madeline raised her hand and summoned Heloise to her side, who held a little handbag in her lap.

"Heloise is a chemist, as you know," Madeline told everyone. "She is here to help us."

George recognized Heloise's little white tabs, and, too, her priestess's way of administering them. These people were always the same, as if they'd studied their mannerisms and movements at some mystic neuro-monastery where it was spiritual to damage your brain. Of course, Heloise herself couldn't really believe it, George told me—a chemist? She would know how, at a dose of four hundred micrograms, this unique serotonergic psychedelic, synthesized by activating lysergic acid and reacting it with diethylamine, would excite the anion of glutamic acid in the brain, bind itself selectively to certain serotonin receptors, and *agonize*—this was the word, George assured me—the D2 dopamine receptor. It wasn't God or the universe, only neurochemistry, like shaking a snow globe and watching the little flakes of silver swirl and excite themselves. It was just a way to lie to your senses. Yet he knelt all the same. He accepted this communion with others, and Heloise's hand on his forehead as she paused, as he closed his eyes, as he felt her move on. It was this way with everyone, George told me. They simply accepted.

"What was it you were going to tell us, Jacques?" Madeline asked, once everyone had received their sacrament.

Jacques didn't move. He didn't look at them at all. "Just that I went outside and the stars began to go out. Then the moon. Everything was dark. And since the moon doesn't burn, it meant—"

Victoria laughed. "That's it? That's the whole dream, then?"

"Yes, that's it."

⸻

Madeline announced a twenty-minute break. She called it this, as though they were laborers on her clock. I know what you're thinking, George told me—that we all joined a cult. But she was just organized, a planner. It must never be forgotten that Madeline Morrison cultivated mysteries and experiences as much as people.

To cultivate is, if not to control, to influence—yes, admittedly to manipulate. She's who I always picture, George told me, when someone uses the English idiom *pull some strings*. She was always pulling strings, the kind that moved your limbs or bobbed your head yes and no or *I don't know, Madeline*; the kind that made you say a thing, a phrase she'd taped into your mind.

Just as George was about to close the bathroom door, Jack stopped him. "Mind if we go together? Whatever she gave us is hitting me already." He stepped inside and locked the door. "You weren't followed, were you?" he said, and laughed at his awful joke. It wasn't that different from a row of urinals, George supposed, to stand adjacent, even if they aimed into the same bowl and, in their intimacy, more freely enjoyed what they saw. Jack's wasn't that different from the last cock that had ruined his life, a plump, springy weight like a roll of wheaty dough warmed up in the heat of one's hands. Why did they have so much power? What had gone wrong in his body or brain that made him so vulnerable to such a ridiculous thing? "Why don't you shake it for me," Jack suggested, and he did.

George went to rejoin Madeline. At least hers was a familiar frustration, a gentle cruelty. But Jack wouldn't let him go. "Let's step out for a smoke, George. I'm feeling pretty good."

"I think I am all right, Jack."

"Nonsense, step outside. I insist."

The night had grown shockingly cold and had driven everyone else from the terrace. Las Vegas and its concrete had run out of yesterday's heat and there was nothing left to warm them, and George shivered as he offered Jack a cigarette. "Thank you for remembering my case," he said. He felt suddenly reckless, as if the glow stretching across the mountains were an ending, a destination. So he touched Jack on the shoulder and said, "It was very kind of you to bring it from the room. Where was it?"

Jack didn't respond. He leaned his elbows on the railing and surveyed the horizon. They were looking north and could see the edge of this tiny, neon city, and the dark of the desert that stretched out after it. If given the right shove, George told me, Jack could have tumbled over the edge. Perhaps with the lights inside, and the shimmering of the curtains, no one would see it, and he could tell them all, yes, it was just horrible, he never would have expected, never would have believed, but there it was, there he went, the things that drugs make people do—and so forth.

George stepped closer. "Usually I keep it on my desk. The case. I enjoy cigarettes while I'm working, as you know. There's really no better way to clear the mind. Is that where it was?"

"George, I'm not going to play that game with you. I know you know. I'm not as inept as you might think."

"And yet you—yet we, so many times—"

"I wanted to tell you, a dozen times, a hundred times even. But you wouldn't understand and none of this would've worked. We wouldn't be here if I'd told you."

"What are you telling me?"

"Well." Jack plucked his handkerchief from his pocket and mopped his forehead. Sweating in the icy night, George thought—so it wouldn't be long at all. "I think we're all about to find out, so it isn't much of a secret anymore."

"For God's sake, Jack."

"Madeline and Walt." He gestured inside, as though George had forgotten they were here or where they were. "I know they're your friends, George. But they're terrorists. Spies. They're incredibly dangerous people, and I think you know it. They're going to get millions of people killed. The Rosenbergs all over again."

"Millions of people," George said, and laughed.

"Why do you think we're here, George? Don't you know where Vegas is?"

"Jack, I think you're having a psychotic reaction. I have seen this before." He knew it wasn't psychosis, but he didn't want any part of this; he wanted to give Jack a way out, to undo this indiscretion. "It's only a drug. You're going to be all right."

"It's not drugs, George. I know how to handle myself. And I'm definitely not crazy. I'm talking about Madeline and Walt, people who want to hurt the world, who want to hurt good people like you and me."

"Why would Madeline and Walt want to hurt anyone? They're kind people, Jack. If perhaps a little—"

"It's human nature, George. We all *want* to hurt people. It's just that some of us know better and some of us don't. Some of us know we're animals and that we need to be restrained. And some of us just want to watch everything burn and be done with it. Nobody really wants to do good or make the world better, we just know that we *have* to."

"Human nature," George said. "I see."

"Animals. Animals is all we are, and every minute we're tempted to prove it. Like you and me, what we do—animals. Don't we know better? Of course we do. But can we resist? Apparently not. Human nature, to take what we want."

"And to give."

Jack didn't care about giving. He waved his hand and turned back to the horizon. Dawn wasn't far away at all. George looked up and saw that most stars had vanished. Venus had risen, like

the sun's scout—*It's this way, this way to daylight,* she might say.
She shimmered, then, as if dropped into a clear pool of water, and
came closer. Was it really so hot, that much closer to the sun, that
a whole planet could be molten, that she could drop sulfurous
lead from the sky? It began to rain stars and George shut his eyes.
When he opened them, he saw nothing but a bright star over the
rosy sediment in the east. Madeline and Walt weren't harmless—
George knew this. But they weren't the Rosenbergs. They weren't
here to sell anything, not secrets and not a politics. Jack had the
wrong idea, and so did whoever was slipping him a little extra
money to rat out his friends and his coworkers.

"I wish you had told me," he said, but Jack was no longer listening.

"George, the building is moving. Is this what she planned?"

"We need to get inside, Jack. We're starting to feel it. It'll be
okay." He put his hand on Jack's shoulder, the last time they'd ever
touch, and led him back into the salon.

"What happened with Ellman?" George whispered before they
sat down.

"You don't think that was me? Ellman was a commie who put
a gun in his mouth. He didn't need any help. The studio was onto
him, and he had no plan B." Then his eyes changed, dilating as if
they'd just noticed George was there, in real life, the conversation
was really happening. "Who the hell do you think I am?"

There wasn't time to answer. The room heaved with sweat and
humming, people tapping their own frequencies. Drugs are not
mystical, George reminded himself. They are not magic. Whatever
happens—it's just a lie.

Everyone and their convictions, he told me—how instead we'd
all destroyed ourselves.

"Let's lock those doors," Madeline was saying. "We don't want

to risk anyone going outside." Walt and Houghton worked together to lock and bar the patio doors, the door to the penthouse
vestibule. They were trapped, or perhaps safe. "Thank you for
being here," Madeline said again. "Thank you for coming. What
we're about to see is real. What you're about to feel is real. I've been
thinking a great deal about our lives, about our species. Do you
know that we adapt? Yes, yes, we do. Do you know that we love?
It's so easy to be cynical about love. To even despair. Let's sit. No,
let's kneel. I want us all to kneel here, on the floor, facing these
windows. This is north. It's almost dawn. It happens just prior to
dawn, like they're trying to outdo it, to prove they don't need it,
that we don't need it. They want dear Jacques's nightmare to come
true, but it will never come true. What I want you all to know is
that I love you, and always have, and that what we've shared is real,
and that how we lived was real. We all meant something. I always
thought the end should feel good. I always thought it should be
something to embrace and not fear. These are lessons I've had to
learn, I've had to teach myself. Walt and I—we understand now.
We know there's nothing we can do, there's nothing anyone can
do. Our warrants are signed. Our contracts are up. I want you to
love that. You should be able to love that. Now just look, and wait,
and watch. I want you to see what I've seen. Nobody blink."

   She was right, George told me. It really was just before dawn
when the flash lit up the last of the night and swept from the testing field seventy miles away to their eyes in a microsecond. No one
would ever unsee it. A light that bright would float on the black
pools of their eyes forever, every time they blinked. Soon they made
sense of it; the light became a shape, and the great white sphere of
it rose and paled into a yellow and then smoldered into orange,
into red, a star born and burning and dying as they worshiped its

entire life in only moments. Then the rumble of it. It wasn't anything like thunder, not thunder's creep and suggestion, thunder's
way of yawning before it roars. It simply arrived and went through
them and moved on, like a roller sweeping a beach. They were too
far away to see the shockwave, but soon after they could see the
cloud. It was distinct, George told me. You'd never confuse it with
anything, that canopy of fire atop a pillar of smoke and dust—
mankind shaking its fist at God while God watched. And of course
people were screaming. Whatever they saw, they each saw it differently. They each understood differently. That's what she'd done to
them, not brought them together but taken them apart, isolated
them from each other. It was them and Madeline, not them and
each other, George told me. And Madeline knew it. She wanted
it. People clawed at the doors. One woman broke glass. A man bit
into his own flesh. Someone tried to swallow a candlestick until
it was taken away. Houghton buried himself under a couch cush-
ion. Jacques was staring out at the burned desert as though he'd
forgotten he was alive. And Jack—Jack had collapsed and covered
his face with his hands and was screaming, his body convulsing
with terror. Then he began to choke, vomiting up gin and bile with
a deep guttural groan like a killed animal. Just an animal, George
thought. A stupid creature doing what creatures did, what they all
did: cowered, cried, asked God for forgiveness, and tried helplessly
to get away or die. Madeline walked over. She knelt and touched
his forehead as he trembled on the floor, and she asked him, "Is
this what you were looking for, Mr. Turner?"

Paris

YESTERDAY, THE SKY TURNED A NEW SHADE OF RED. Canada was burning—this was how the articles described it. For days we'd smelled the smoke, and by then we were so accustomed to wearing masks that it was second nature to put it on when we stepped outside. The day before, everything had worn a tinge of copper, and the sun itself looked like someone's lone, lost penny at the bottom of a sink stopped with a rusty drain. Now, we woke on a different planet—the deep and dark red, as one imagines, of Mars. My husband and I took photographs and sent them to our friends, who sent us photos of their own as if to confirm: yes, this is how it is. And that's what I wondered. *What if this is how it is now? What do we do?* Presumably, we'd do what we did: make coffee, fry the eggs, turn on the radio, kiss one another when we crossed paths in the kitchen, and peel the last of the summer blood oranges, which—perhaps the trick of all last things—always seemed the sweetest. A young friend of ours came over and panicked; it was the end of the world and there would be no future. We made him a drink. "Nothing like this has ever happened before," he said, which seemed true enough to agree with, and, a bit tipsy, we put on our masks and went for a walk. Everyone was out. People stopped and spoke to each other. They pointed at the horizon and were all very friendly. This morning, the color is already beginning to clear. I thought, *They've done it again, George. They almost got us.*

═══

He left. Not only that house and Madeline and Jacques but California. Its people were annihilated in a way no one seemed to mind. She may have given him that, this vision of a dead land, in her radical nihilism. The fact is, she was right: he never forgot it. At any moment, in any setting, it could come to him without warning and vivid as the morning he'd seen it, the same burning of the sun before the sun even arrived. It wasn't something you could go back to, a life where that had happened, a life you'd *seen* the end of. And she'd known it—or at least sensed it. Greedy as she was, she did recognize in others their potential, and maybe George, in her eyes, was the kind of person who got away, who had a life he didn't know about waiting someplace for him to live it. After all, he imagined her saying—he told me he could conjure her voice at will, so singular of a person she'd been—after all, you already got away twice, didn't you, George? He'd never spoken with her about Budapest, and certainly never much about New York other than where he'd lived and what he'd done for money (people like Madeline were always interested in how people like George paid for things), but she had seen his runaway's eyes, his fugitive's soul. *Maybe,* he could hear her saying, *you'll survive us all.*

New York was not the same. No city ever is. He took an apartment off Riverside Drive and kept it faintly monastic—books, a writing table, a bed, a chair for reading—and went out. To listen to jazz, he told me, or drink coffee, or walk along the river. It snowed in New York. Every so often it would just happen and it caught him on the street, or had suddenly arrived when he surfaced from the subway. It rained, too, and in the spring and summer, George knew, the sky would offer thunderstorms. It was often unpleasant, one way or another, and people let him hear about it. They talked about it, this weather. They said more than "It's windy" or "It's still."

Yvette got him a job through an editor she knew, at least if György—*I'm sorry, George?*—at least if George didn't mind working with art critics. All he'd have to do was green their columns, she said. "They always go on too long, these art people, and something has to get cut. You'll get a knack for it pretty quick." She looked into his eyes as she took a deep drag and puffed it out slowly, to cloud her vision, or maybe his perception of her. "I've missed you," she said, and he didn't bother to pretend she hadn't just made him cry.

He did develop a knack, as Yvette promised, and in a year he was making enough to live. A doctor in the Village thought Dexedrine was a cure-all, and George had no trouble, when he wished, staying up for a few days and revising his essay. Yes, he said—he still carried it around and cut it apart and pieced it back together. It still haunted him, even if the revolution that inspired it had long been squashed, its leaders betrayed and executed. We want to burn, George said, to be disintegrated—wasn't it obvious? Even Madeline had understood this, and had tried to show us, to make us understand. Her embrace of annihilation wasn't evil; it was sad. She'd become so lost, and what he hoped, in twenty or so pages, was to articulate a way back, though she was likely never to see it herself. There had to be a way back, he thought, for those who find their god in fire.

In 1958, he saw a flimsy adaptation of *Winesburg, Ohio* that didn't last long on Broadway, but that wasn't Madeline's fault at all. She was superb, he told me, as captivating as she'd ever been—and as expressive. While the audience was less than enthused, the cast took their bows, and smiled, and mouthed *thank you* as if the house were thundering, and Madeline especially seemed to bask in this imagined, fantasy praise as she blew kisses and clasped her hands and curtsied before she took her exit. George walked home through the snow, a blustery kind of stratospheric dust that stung at his eyes, and thought it was best not to commune with who he'd been. In Madeline's heart she carried around a George and he carried around a Madeline and where each was it wasn't cold, it wasn't so dark and finished. Neither deserved to lose that companion, not now.

Destruction is illuminating in man's ethical darkness. It lights the path, the same path we walk toward creation. Somebody finally published it, one of those little magazines you always saw stacked on the tanks of toilets in professors' apartments, and that was that. No one sent letters to G. W. Kurtz, the "writer living in New York," and no one approached or solicited him for more work. No one, as far as George knew, read a damn word of it. They paid him twenty-five dollars and said they were proud to have it, they'd never read anything quite like it, he should definitely send more work in the future. He never did. You get old, he told me—and I smiled, because the version of himself he narrated was scarcely thirty—you get old and silence accumulates. Like any accumulation, like any ongoingness, to diminish or interrupt it feels like a failure, a violation against oneself. I suppose it's what a Catholic would call sin, to throw away one's silence.

Everything had begun to change, as if the island itself and its million people had further floated ever so slightly out to sea. There were nights he was turned away from the jazz clubs, and when he wasn't, the mood had deepened. Yes, the playing was more passionate, more exuberant, sweatier and achier, but there was, too, some fury underneath it. All over the city, people distributed pamphlets; there was a genus of politics or ideology for everyone, and so niche you needed a dictionary to decrypt it. No one thought they were going to live. He learned the smell of heroin, the city's dimmest hallways rank with a braided tang of cooked licorice and cat piss. Art was no longer about color or brushstroke or drip or stain, but about statement—even if there was no statement. *It just is*, the critics liked to write in their drafts; it was always the first line George cut. Who cared if a thing was? What mattered was *how* it was, and nothing was how it used to be. Something was misaligned. There was a gratitude, he said, in not being there, sitting among the artists and the poets as they drank and fought; undeniably it was a hell he could no longer love. The lonely life: it was at least his life.

And there were movies. Even if he didn't think about them in the same way, they, too, were changing, but for the better. Perhaps it was simply that painting and poetry were finished but cinema had just begun—a cliché, he said, "I know that now, but that's really how it seemed." In the summer, with fewer art openings, there was less work at the magazine, and he spent his afternoons in the dark. It was the only way he enjoyed growing older. There was so much chatter in those days. Going to the movies was the only language George *wanted* to learn, the only one that enticed and beckoned him. "That's exactly how I used to feel, George," Yvette told him as they walked through the Modern. "About painting, I mean, way back when. Of course people had been painting for thousands of years, so it's a bit silly to compare it to a technology that's only a few decades old, but you understand me? It *felt* like it had never happened until it came to me. It's just like being in love."

In 1960, he found a reason to leave. It was a young director's feature debut. He was nearly the same age as George and had spent years writing for a French film magazine; then he decided, so he told interviewers, to abandon essays and criticize film with film. What shock does in art, George said, is that it puts you *there*. And this film put him there. He wanted to be in the one place in the world it seemed possible for this to happen, for the next George to be created.

There wasn't much to arrange. He packed his clothes, his Olivetti, the books Paul had given him, his letters, and bought a second-class ticket for Cherbourg. In those days, he said, it was much easier (which makes me laugh to write this now, thirty-four years after we last spoke, because in those days—the days I sat with him as he told me this story—it, too, was so much easier). No one fussed over his passport or pulled him aside or arrested him, and in a little over a week, he said, he was in Paris. He took a room in a hotel that smelled of licorice and cat piss—a little reminder of home, he said, and wheezed with a laugh—and began to walk.

Perhaps that was what had never worked about Los Angeles. He didn't drive, and never would. A horrible invention, he called it. But a city like that had required a car, or at least some man with a car to pull up and honk outside your apartment. But it wasn't any way to live in a place. We have a speed, George said, and it's the correct one. We see at that speed, and listen, and untangle what we smell. "I am in Paris," he said to himself, a cherished disbelief. He was back in what they called the Old World, which felt staggeringly new—and young, as young as New York was when he was young. Every once in a while he felt a shudder as Budapest passed through him—the shadow beneath a bench in a park, the unique tang of sewer gas not far from the Seine. This was the same Europe as that Europe, the same Europe in which his parents had raised him to learn the names of flowers and of birds. It had suffered the same wars and suffered its own version of an uprising, George said, even if these new revolutionaries, as they called themselves, were students, and George, at that time, was forty, and the newspapers watched them with a detached fascination, with only a little horror as the president fled the country, and it was all, in the end, a little game against the greater apocalypse of what some said was the collapse of what some called, wistfully, the West—Vietnam and Kent State, firebombings and riots and cacophonous music, self-immolations, drugs and assassinations and "race questions," napalmed bodies advertised on television, museum exhibits of gunshot wounds and rape scenes. It was the end of days, they said, but then there were more days. Nothing was going to end or be reborn, everyone knew that. And before long it was the 1970s.

For a decade now, George had written for the same magazine he'd learned about through this young director—one of the most famous directors, now, in the world. He'd met him only once and found him petulant and dismissive, mischievous without charm, and tried not to hold this against his work. But it did diminish it— and that is your lesson, George told me, not to meet the people you respect. Because you don't respect them at all, only their work. But it was a good living, writing these essays and reviews, interviewing the occasional filmmaker, editing the work of younger writers, and it paid for a good life: an afternoon in front of a single painting, if he wanted; a table to himself with a jar of rillettes, some grilled bread, and a bottle of Morgon; a paper cone of chestnuts on a drizzly evening, bought from the family who parked themselves at the end of Rue Lecuirot; inviting a man up to his apartment and not caring, not worrying, who might see him leave. There were little trips out into the country, or trains to Milan and Rome and Naples. A flight to Berlin to take pictures, he said, of the wall to see if it was really there, that it wasn't a metaphor. I know this all sounds romantic, George told me, but it really *was* romantic. It was a romance I didn't know I needed. Besides, he said, it wasn't all roses. Paris is cold—you know this—and there's never any way to get warm. People have stolen from me. I was attacked once—did I ever tell you?—in the toilets at the Gare du Nord. It wasn't serious, but it did rattle me for a year or two, but eventually I got over it and now that's all in the past.

And then he met Jean-Marc.

There is very little to say of joy, George said. It may be that's what's so special about it, that it's nondescript, even banal. They met through a local theater, and then had dinner, and then went to George's apartment, and they saw each other again, and then lived together for eleven years.

This was the seventies, George told me. It was all becoming so normal, so vogue. "In addition to the usual, horrible names, people began to call us sweet and lovely. We lived together and made meals and went to dinners and art openings. I never reviewed the plays he appeared in, but I did what I could to support them, to support him." George did, however, inadvertently get Jean-Marc his first part in a film, and thereafter it was easier for them both to buy something for the apartment or take a month in Capri or—George's favorite—spend an entire summer at Jean-Marc's mother's house in the hills south of Aix. It had been decades, he said, since he'd been around anyone's mother, and he remembered how nervous he was, how terrified, the first time they'd gone. Even with Jean-Marc's assurances—*She'll love you* and *She doesn't mind* and *She's always known*—George thought he'd somehow estrange this young man and ruin his life. But Marguerite was kind. She cooked for them. She showed them how to milk the ewe and how to spot a hen hiding a fresh egg. In her Citroën she took them to buy fish and oysters at the markets in Marseille, and to chateaus where they loaded her trunk with crates of Mourvèdre and Cinsault. On Sundays, people from the village enjoyed her generosity, her company. It was her great pleasure just to cook for people, even if she'd never do it for money. They'd arrive in their cars just a little before noon, George said, and set up their tables or their blankets and unpack their own dishes, and often they brought their own wine, and some gift to leave behind, which they always had to hide because Marguerite was adamant against gifts. And she invited George and Jean-Marc to talk with these neighbors and their families, to sit down and have lunch as she moved from family to family and gave them bread and ewe's cheese, olives, and passed around a terrine that'd been aged a few days. Game was the favorite, hare and boar and a little squab—often the same animals these neighbors hid in her larder (with Jean-Marc's collaboration) as gifts. "My sons," she said as she introduced them, and left the conclusion—brothers who looked nothing alike, or lovers she'd agreed to recognize—up to these Provençales, who didn't seem to care either way.

Once, she pulled George aside and said, "You know, he was always so skittish, even a little unhappy, as though there was something he could see that I couldn't, some doom—am I making my point?" Her fingers were long and slender despite their strength, their years pounding pastry dough and wrangling farm animals and tearing flesh to shreds, and George watched them close over his own hands. "You are welcome here whenever you like, as long as you like."

Marguerite, he told me, was almost as hard to lose as Jean-Marc himself. She still called, now and then—I knew this because I'd spoken to her, I'd heard her voice, the loneliness in it as she asked for George, as she told me to tell him he was still welcome in Provence, that she would love to see him, that losing Jean-Marc didn't mean she would, or could bear, losing another son. But George shook his head as he overheard. "She can't see me like this," he said. "Not after what she saw Jean-Marc go through. It wouldn't be fair, by any means."

"Does she even know, George?"

"She has assumed. It's safe to assume it'll happen to us all, is it not?"

A GRAVE IN THE CLOUDS

There is, I think, in every life that streak of happiness like a star's scratch across the night. It isn't planned and it cannot last but it does arrive, and you either notice it or don't. George did; and he was grateful, he told me, that I was there to see it right as it faded, that I saw the tail end of its burning trail. To see someone experience joy, he said—it tells you everything you need to know about a person, perhaps because it's so rare to witness.

I met George and Jean-Marc at a bookstore off Rue d'Alésia. They'd come to see an American poet who mumbled and swayed, old and finished, like a sleepy house cat twitching its tail. I'd only been in Paris for two months, a semester abroad that turned into twenty years. They cared for each other and said things casually— about literature, about painting, about movies—I thought a person could transcribe directly into a book and call it profound. At first it was physical—I was young and they liked having me—but then I, too, began to learn and to say things that no longer made them laugh or roll their eyes but think, but take me seriously. I brought them music they'd never heard before. We argued about who would end up in books and who would be erased before the century's end.

We played euchre; my grandmother had taught me, back in Michigan, and George thought it was the most ridiculous, wonderful way to waste an evening. They loved museums and took me with them so Jean-Marc had someone to talk to when George got lost. You'd see him smile every now and then, George, as he recognized a painting at the other end of a gallery. I thought, If this was what life was when you got older, if there were memories waiting for you all over the world—all kinds of friends hidden in objects or pictures or places—I thought, This can't really be so bad, can it?

They were my models, if it isn't too embarrassing to say. They had books on their shelves and art on their walls and they loved each other. In our youth, we really don't need much. "Mon petit ragoût," Jean-Marc called him—that was enough for me. If I picture this, Jean-Marc is sitting on the sofa in the apartment. Back then, the living room is full of plants—Jean-Marc's "children," who require a great deal of his time and attention and to whom George is happy to defer if it means more time reading, more time glancing up at some muted movie on the television. But now, Jean-Marc is calling to him—"Ragoût, where are the little blue plates we bought in Portugal?"—and George is rolling his eyes; he's never liked being interrupted, not when he's talking to "our guest."

"But it isn't a guest, it's just the nephew. Get in here and help me. You've hidden the plates because you think they're ugly."

"They're hideous, but I'd never hide them."

"Come find them."

While they had their little fight—it was never anything serious—I thumbed through the rack of records. I thought someday I would be old (as I considered them then) and I would have a man and we'd have surrounded ourselves with a life, and I thought, Well, it can wait. I had plans, of course. Ideas. Like most young people I didn't realize my life had already begun and that I was living it quickly. I didn't realize, not until much later, that George, too, had assumed all these things would wait, that they'd simply fall into your lap while you did your work, the real work, the life's work. "You don't want to be like me," he told me, a common refrain in those earlier days. "You don't want to wake up every day and think, I've wasted my life, and then drink some coffee, read a book, kiss your husband, have a sandwich, and smoke a dozen cigarettes before it comes right back, that thought. What have I done, anyway?"

When they found the plates, Jean-Marc brought us his little invention, a sort of amuse-bouche made from radishes and mustard. They were terrible.

"Did you follow the recipe?" George asked him. "Or are your eyes bothering you again?"

"You know there's no recipe. And besides, your eyes are going to go first, old stringy ragoût. You'll be my sweet blind old man and I'll read to you, like we always used to see de Beauvoir—do you remember?—reading the papers to Sartre in the Deux Magots." Jean-Marc turned to me. "They were always there, those two. He nodded along when she read, like a fat little vulture. It was so sweet." He turned back to George and kissed him on the forehead. "One day you'll be *my* fat little vulture. My old blind jelly."

They traveled. There were stories in the objects on their shelves. A cat named Paul slunk around and loved no one but George, and with whom George was uncharacteristically, even childishly affectionate. One day, I learned that George was called ragoût because, on the second night they had dinner together, George had come down with a head cold and sneezed into his stew. This was the kind of story that made Jean-Marc light up and laugh while George blushed, petting Paul as if he weren't listening; it was the kind of thing that made me feel so young compared to their ancient history together, which—as I've said—was only eleven years. Because it wasn't long after I met them that we watched Jean-Marc die and took care of him together, that George read to him for hours because it was Jean-Marc, not George, who'd gone blind. Then George began to die. "I suppose no one gets to survive twice," he told me, and gestured to the Broussais Hospital, whose smokestacks we could see from the window and which right then were exhaling one more of us into the sky. He turned to me. "I really should have done something with my life." But no matter how many times he told me to go, to live, to get out, to escape, I shrugged and made him tea or soup, or sorted his medications, or simply read him poems by the window. And I listened, as I think I've made clear.

It was in April of 1986, when the Chernobyl nuclear plant melted down and spewed radiation over hundreds of miles, that George told me, "I've been waiting thirty years for this." He was only half-serious, but then he told me about that party, about Madeline, about those days of revolution in 1956. It was the first I'd heard about Jack, who turned out to be a sort of convert. Madeline really had known what she was doing. She'd known, too, that Jack didn't have the temperament; he certainly wasn't KGB, as George had feared, only a civilian informant with an unfortunate, stupid patriotism. He was only harmful, Madeline had known, in the way that a big clumsy animal is harmful, a beast with no idea what it's doing. In the early sixties, Jack tried to blow up a government building and went to prison for ten years. He took that night very seriously. She'd radicalized him with a single act—you can't get much more precise than that. When he got out, he joined the antiwar movement. He moved to San Francisco and raised money for people brutalized by the police, ran for office and lost, started a newspaper devoted to taking down Ronald Reagan, and found a man of his own. We spoke on the phone, George told me. Can you believe that? He found me and called me—who knows who did him what favor, nobody was supposed to know where I was—but he did. Maybe he did have a little talent after all. He said, "You'll never guess what I'm up to, George," and he was right, George couldn't guess at all. "I really owe you one, George. You didn't know it, you had no idea, but you gave me a whole new life. And I wanted to tell you that before I said goodbye." It was very sweet of him, George said. There was still so much Jack in his voice, even if so much had changed.

"That was months ago," George told me. "Even if I'm optimistic, I have to assume he's gone, too."

We're always waiting, it seems. I'm not trying to be profound or give you some kind of koan—you who will see far more, far worse than I, as it's increasingly clear. In those early days nobody could give you a straight answer about Chernobyl. Was the whole earth contaminated? Had radiation seeped into us all, and would we all get sick and have the flesh slough off our bones like it did from those who'd been there, or from those who'd seen Hiroshima wiped from the earth? Would we die of cancer like those in Vegas, over the years, or in southern Utah, both downwind of the bombs Madeline loved to watch explode at dawn from the suite she never relinquished, not even after they banned atmospheric testing? Would the sky, once red, always be red?

It wouldn't comfort George to know that Madeline moved there after Walt died, that she sold her house in Malibu and never left Vegas again. The reclusive actress of the desert, they called her, even though she had countless visitors and went out among the gamblers in her sunglasses, her white hair wrapped in silk. It may not even comfort him, were he still here, to know that Madeline would die gracefully and quietly and very, very old in that same room, watching over that same desert, where she had welcomed death in its impersonal swiftness. Where she had offered herself as death's evangelist yet outlived them all. I never met her. I didn't want to. I knew, from George, just how charming she could be.

The bomb didn't fall, of course, not in the way she meant. And Chernobyl, ultimately, didn't reach all that far. Fukushima contaminated the entire Pacific Ocean but we're still eating its fish. Is it immoral to lose hope? I've seen it happen and I don't think so, but then I don't think even the hopeless are really lost. Madeline thought she had arrived. George thought he had arrived. How must it feel to know the earth is going on without you? I want to know if their souls can see us. I want to know if they can hear me, if they are eavesdropping on our despair. It must be so sad to die, to feel yourself miss out on everything that will come after, even if there are still bombs and diseases and disasters, even if people do get murdered and beaten, if they die in unspeakable pain, if it is still a fact that some live with their damaged bodies, or simply their aged bodies, bodies that were once beautiful and now are not. But at least they lived, at least they had their time, and I imagine that's what people like Madeline and George had prepared themselves for, had convinced themselves to believe—that there would be no more bodies at all, that there would be no more of anything. You have to understand them, even if you don't want to. Their ghosts must be so ashamed—and is that any way to be dead?

Listen: that you lived never needs to be forgiven. You both did what you had to do. You loved who you had to love. Your gift, your life, was an entire planet. You traveled here and looked around, you tried the food, you talked to people, you took your pleasure, and you left.

Notes

p. 10:   the correct *Paradise Lost* line is "From my clay," not *thy*

p. 98:   quotes are from Tennessee Williams's "An Appreciation," written in 1948 for a group exhibition at Kootz Gallery

p. 109:   these details about Auschwitz and Buchenwald can be found in Mary Gabriel's extraordinary *Ninth Street Women*

p. 110:   "It made angels out of everybody" is a direct quote from Willem de Kooning's "What Abstract Art Means to Me" (1951); "Their eyes melted in ecstasy" is adapted from "The eyes that actually saw the light melted out of sheer ecstasy," from the same essay

p. 117:   Paul's observations on color are inspired by Max Kozloff's 1967 essay, "Venetian Art and Florentine Criticism," published in *Artforum*

p. 130:   the newsreel described is #526, released by Universal Pictures Company on August 5, 1946

p. 172:   the philosopher is Hannah Arendt

p. 207:   the detail about the Broussais Hospital is from Hervé Guibert's journals: "I had never noticed that I could see the turret of the Broussais Hospital crematorium from my windows. Suddenly I believed in a fire, a very black smoke rose, then more and more gray and transparent, I looked at the body that was disappearing into the sky" (trans. Nathanaël)

Acknowledgments

To everyone at Counterpoint, thank you so much for making this book everything I wanted it to be and more—especially Dan Smetanka, whose love for the novel really made me believe in it and whose careful edits saved me from going a little too far; and to Farjana Yasmin and Nicole Caputo for such a beautiful cover. Thank you to everyone who read this book, copyedited and proofed it, passed it around, designed it, showed it to people, and tried to convince everyone to buy it or read it. Authors, readers, and the entire publishing industry couldn't exist without you, and you all deserve a union and a lot more money.

Thank you to Erik Hane, whose support for and belief in this book from the very beginning encouraged me that maybe it wasn't such a bad idea after all; and to Laura Zats, who read it carefully and asked some difficult questions that gave me a few healthy nightmares.

I'm so grateful for my earliest readers, Hunter and CJ, whose enthusiasm helped me work up the courage to send it to my agent.

Thank you to Dawn Frederick, who convinced me maybe I should be writing novels after all.

Thank you to Michael, without whom I wouldn't be here.

And thank you to my favorite diner, The Bad Waitress (RIP) on 26th and Nicollet in Minneapolis, whose old sci-fi film posters hung on the walls made me wonder who wrote such movies, and why.

PATRICK NATHAN is the author of *Image Control* and *Some Hell*, a finalist for the Lambda Literary Award. His short fiction and essays have appeared in *The New Republic*, *American Short Fiction*, *Gulf Coast*, *The Baffler*, and elsewhere. He lives in Minneapolis. Find out more at patricknathan.com.